A BEAUTIFUL GIRL

"Cassandra Ulrich's *A Beautiful Girl* is a compelling story of a young woman caught in an abusive home life and her journey to overcome its chains. Ulrich takes on this delicate storyline with style and sensitivity that draws the readers immediately into her complex, yet identifiable, characters' world. She's definitely an up-and-coming author with plenty to offer."

— Suzanne Y. Snow, Author of the *Forrorrois* Series

"*A Beautiful Girl* starts off with an unusual, two-person perspective; it allows the reader to see the story through the filter of both an abused teenage girl and a teenage boy who, like most teenage boys, struggles with confidence. You see the two teens' point of view of the story, and even though you're reading essentially the same story, it holds your interest by revealing the thoughts of both, something we all wish we could do better! Cassandra Ulrich has a feel for many of the struggles of young teens, both the common and the hidden ones that no one talks about."

— Kurt Smith, Owner and author of Ballpark E-Guides

"*A Beautiful Girl* lends its voice to the countless nameless victims of abuse silenced by shame. Cassandra Ulrich uses a youthful perspective to tell a story that is bound to capture the attention of young readers."

— Kiana Jones-Peoples, Avid Reader

CASSANDRA ULRICH

A BEAUTIFUL GIRL

☙

Cassandra Ulrich • PO Box 492, Collingswood, NJ 08108-0492 • cassulrich@gmail.com • http://cassandraulrich.blogspot.com/ • http://cassandraulrich.com/ • This book is a work of fiction. Any references to historical events, real people, or real locales are used fictitiously. Other names, characters, places, and incidents are products of the author's imagination, and any resemblance to actual events or locales or persons, living or dead, is entirely coincidental. • Copyright © 2011 by Cassandra Ulrich. • All rights reserved, including the right of reproduction in whole or in part in any form. • Book design by Celeste McKenzie • The text for this book is set in New Times Roman • Manufactured in the United States of America • Library of Congress Cataloging-in-Publication Data • Cassandra Ulrich • A Beautiful Girl/ Cassandra Ulrich. 1st ed. • p. cm. • Summary: A girl befriends a boy at school who helps her escape abuse by her step-father. • ISBN-13: 978-0-692-27778-2 • (1. Parental abuse. 2. Boy meets girl. 3. High School. 4. Inspirational. 5. Contemporary Teen Issues)

10 9 8 7 6 5 4

To Sarah M. who was indeed a Beautiful girl
and
to Jackie G., elsewhere but not forgotten.
To all the Beautiful Girls and Boys.

AUTHOR'S NOTE

God – for creating beauty in all of us.

Family – Thanks to Ernest for being my Rick throughout the years of our marriage, to my sons for their love of fun in life. Henry and Anne, my parents, for valuing education and love of music. Ethel, my mother-in-law, for your encouraging words. My sister Bernadine for expressing how my story can be useful to help many, and her daughter Nefertari for, well, you know. Thanks.

Alice and Demian – for reading my rough draft and being moved deeply by the characters and the story. Barrie – for answering my many questions about bus schedules and homeroom etiquette. Her son Charlton – for beta reading my partially corrected manuscript and alerting me of what's cool and what's not.

Joyce, Robin, Kurt, and Kiana – for your encouragement to keep writing.

My author friends Ken, Suzanne, and Susan – for your much appreciated advice. Laurie – for your insight into a mom's relationship with a teenage son.

Melissa of Art Sanctuary – for telling me about the event that led to this novel being published less than six months later and for your enthusiasm. Max – for your humor while editing this book. Thank you for the opportunity to tell this story.

Destiny's Child – for the song "The Story of Beauty". Your song inspired this story years before it was written.

Holy Spirit – for spurring me on to write this story in two months when I would have much preferred to write something less emotionally taxing.

ଔ

A BEAUTIFUL GIRL

SARA'S UGLY SECRET
ᛒ

Hi. My name is Sara Miller, and I'm seventeen years old. I was born in Philadelphia and have lived here all my life. Fortunately, I've always had a place to sleep and food to eat. Only problem is, I don't know who I am.

I used to know what I liked, what I didn't. I used to play and laugh. Now, I don't remember how to laugh. I don't even think I smile much anymore, if at all.

Growing up with a father who played instruments nurtured my love for music. He taught me how to play piano and violin, but now I don't play much. After his death three years ago, my mother remarried, so a lot has changed.

At first, Mom – her name is Bridgette - thought she could make it taking care of four kids on her own. But with the cost of daycare, and no one to look after us at night, going it alone became…a challenge.

So, she remarried after almost two years of struggling to keep a roof over our heads. Without hesitation, my step-father, Chuck Walsh, sold my violin for cash and had forbidden instruments of *any* kind in the house. He wanted nothing within our reach that reminded us of the father we once knew.

That's when my life took a turn for the worse. Chuck started beating Mom almost every night. I always huddled in my bedroom closet with my three younger siblings until it was over. We covered our ears with our hands, but we still heard her screams. We prayed that we wouldn't be next.

But, Chuck's already promised I'll be next. He's only waiting for my eighteenth birthday to "treat you the way I treat my wife". How can I escape this?

Chuck's decided he wants to soften me up, get me ready. He makes me do things I don't want to think about. Sometimes he…*shhh…don't say it, don't think it. It hurts too much…I feel dirty all over.*

Mom says I was the most beautiful baby she'd ever seen, but I don't feel beautiful anymore. How could anyone else see me as beautiful? *I feel so dirty…all over. I didn't ask for this!*

It's my senior year and my first day at a new school. I'm scared. Chuck took us away from our home in Germantown, a place northeast of downtown Philadelphia, to Cherry Hill, New Jersey. He claims the pay is better as a security guard in the Garden State, but I think he's trying to hide us in the suburbs. It's not a horrible place, but it frightens me that I wouldn't know where to run if I need to.

This morning, I said goodbye to my younger siblings, who are also having a hard time with the change, and got on my bus. We made many stops before finally arriving at the school. *My heart seems to be skipping every other beat.*

So many students and I can't make friends with any of them. Chuck promised harsh punishment if any of us grew attached to anyone. As for me, if he ever suspects I like someone, well, my birthday present from him will arrive earlier than expected. I'm trapped in a wide open world. I'm trapped by the man who holds my mother hostage.

I found my locker after an initial stop at the office, and then I headed for my first class, homeroom. I liked that because I had time to get my bearings and pull myself together. I entered the class, but the only available seat was at the back of the class.

Scanning the room, I took in what the girls wore and how happy they seemed. I tried not to notice the boys, but one of them caught my eye. *He's cute.* I looked at my shoes, trying to avoid eye contact as I walked past him. *I can't let myself like anyone here, not even a little.*

I slid into my seat and looked up toward the front of the classroom to find the same boy looking at me. My face felt hot. *Why?* I noticed how warm his brown eyes are before quickly switching my gaze. *Such care is in those eyes.* His gaze reminded me of the way my dad often looked at my mom. *Is that how Mom ended up with Chuck? She forgot what to look for?*

It just so happens, the boy showed up in most of my classes. The teachers called him Rick. Rick.

I made it through all my morning classes. No one approached me and that's fine. It would only cause heartache if I had to reject them later. I didn't want to reject them, but Chuck has never failed to do what he says.

I found the cafeteria. It was easy enough. The noisy conversations coming from a door at the end of the hallway provided the biggest clue. Longing eyes and quick paces were further clues, which betrayed the hunger inside many students that needed to be satisfied.

I paid for my lunch and sat alone at a small table in the corner. I hoped no one would notice me, but to my dismay, I heard footsteps closing in on my location.

"Hi," said a male voice. "You're new here, so I thought I would introduce myself. I'm Rick," he finished, extending his arm for a hand shake, as he smiled at me.

I felt goose bumps pull at the hairs on my arm, and my stomach churned. *Oh, God, this isn't happening. I can't make friends, especially not with him.* But something inside me took over, and before I realized what's happening, I extended my arm toward him and spoke.

"I know. I heard the teachers call on you. Mine's Sara."

"It's good to meet you, Sara. Mind if I sit?"

His brown almond-shaped eyes sparkled and his voice sounded as calming as the surface of a quiet lake. *He looks Asian, but...*

"No," I said, wondering if he noticed my quivering hand as I pulled it back into my lap.

I looked at my food and realized I had lost my appetite. I heard him shift around in his chair.

"I wanted to meet you. You're in most of my classes. Who knows? We might be able to pair up for some of those class projects." He paused. "Sometimes, I have trouble eating the food here, too. You never know what's in there some days. Where're you from?"

"Philly," I replied. "Germantown area."

He's kind and friendly. I looked at him and saw the details of his face. *He has a strong chin.* Scanning his face, I caught a glimpse of two dimples in his cheeks that seemed to mark the ends of his captivating smile.

"Cool. Did you just move here then?" Rick asked, seeming a bit nervous.

"Yes. My parents wanted a change of scenery. Are you from around here?" *I really shouldn't be continuing this conversation. Why didn't I cut it off when he said 'hi'?*

"Yeah. Hey, um, do you wanna do something this weekend? A few of us are going to a party Friday night. I could introduce you to some people."

I felt my arms wrap around my torso.

"I can't." I looked away from his face and then quickly turned back again. I found it difficult not to look at him. I wanted so much to be his friend. I wanted to be free to have just a little piece of happiness.

"Oh, that's too bad. Maybe some other time."

I didn't answer. I think I shrugged.

He finished eating his lunch, seeming at a loss for what else he should say. I nibbled at my plate until he got up.

"There's the bell. We better go. Class starts in five minutes. I can take your tray if you want," offered Rick.

"No, thanks. I got it."

I picked up my tray and walked to the door, throwing my trash away and dropping the tray on the cart. Rick followed me out of the cafeteria, but started walking next to me after we entered the hallway.

We walked in silence to our next class.

Afterwards, I rushed out toward my final class of the day, relieved to find Rick did not have the same class. At the end of the day, I caught him looking inquisitively at me as I got on my bus. *What in the world have I gotten myself into? What am I going to do now?*

When the bus dropped me off, I felt Chuck watching me as I walked up to the front door and went inside. I dared not look at him, in case my face gave something away.

Mom dusted the coffee table. "Hi, honey, how was school today?"

"Fine," I said abruptly before dashing into my room, locking the door, and falling on my bed for a good cry.

RICK NOTICES SARA

ಬಿ

Here I am, Rick Connor, in my last year of high school. I can't believe I go to college next year. I thought about joining the military, but after Dad got killed in a training accident in a mid-East desert, Mom won't even consider letting me do it. So, I'm going to college next year, hopefully, on a music scholarship.

I love to play piano, acoustic guitar, alto saxophone, and violin. This semester is going to get crazy. I have a music recital in December here at school. A number of music schools have been invited to attend. If they love me, I'm in. I'm so nervous about messing something up, so I intend to spend as much time as possible practicing after school in our music room.

My mom's big sister is Aunt Emma. She's a social worker and lives around the corner from Mom and me. Aunt Emma's really cool and I often visit her for advice when I'm too uncomfortable talking to my mom about stuff. She's said a lot to me to help me put this whole music thing into perspective.

I was kind of down the first day of school, though. I thought, man, it's twelfth grade and I don't even have a girlfriend. I think I'm good looking enough, but the girls at school just aren't interested in classical musicians. They want the jocks or the hope-to-be rock stars. So as I drove into the school's parking lot in a car I purchased with money from my summer job, I prayed someone who likes me would come my way.

I saw Taylor, my best friend, running to the front door.

"Wait up," I yelled and hurried toward him. "What's your first period class?"

"After homeroom, I got Physics," replied Taylor.

"I've got AP History after homeroom. I'll have to catch you at lunch then."

"I don't know, Rick. Coach Donovan wants to meet at lunch today. Maybe tomorrow."

"Alright."

We entered homeroom and grabbed our seats. Taylor and I sat, comparing class schedules when the unexpected occurred. A new student entered the room. She had dark brown curls in a braid draped over her left shoulder. She also had a pretty face, not like the typical favored features of cheerleaders, but attractive and easy on the eyes.

She looked around the classroom before turning her head to look straight at me. Her green eyes were surrounded by a saddened countenance.

I wonder why she's sad. I tried to hold her gaze, but she quickly stared at the ground as she walked past me. Up close, I noticed some brown freckles on either side of her button nose. *She looks cute.*

I studied her as she found a seat in the back of the class. I smiled at her when she looked up, causing her olive skin to slightly redden. I finally released her from my gaze when she turned away once more.

When the teacher took attendance, I learned that her name is Sara, such a sweet name for a pretty girl. After homeroom, I became pleasantly surprised to see her in most of my morning classes. *What luck! Now, it's lunchtime and a chance to introduce myself to her.*

I just finished paying for my lunch when I saw Sara sitting alone at a small table in the far corner of the cafeteria. I paused to say hi to a few friends before continuing toward Sara. Her body tensed, so I figured I'd better say something before I scared her away completely.

"Hi. You're new here, so I thought I would introduce myself. I'm Rick," I said, balancing my tray on my left palm while offering my hand for a handshake.

Sara offered her hand in return and I took it. *Her hand is soft to touch.*

"I know," she said, her voice quiet, yet clear and sultry.

I don't think she realizes how attractive her voice is. Instead, she seemed somewhat timid, afraid of eye contact. Aunt Emma said there's always a story behind why a person behaves a certain way. I wondered what Sara's story might be.

"I heard the teachers call on you. Mine's Sara."

"It's good to meet you, Sara. Mind if I sit?"

I really hoped she wouldn't mind. I so wanted to sit with the new girl with the pretty freckled face and the dreamy voice. I held my breath until she answered.

"No," she said, and quickly pulled her hand back and placed it in her lap.

I could tell she was nervous about having me here, but I sat across from her trying to think of what to say. I figured I would just say the first thing on my mind and hoped it didn't scare her away.

"I wanted to meet you. You're in most of my classes. Who knows? We might be able to pair up for some of those class projects."

Sara stopped eating. Man, I hope I didn't cause her to lose her appetite. Maybe, I'm nervous too. I can't believe I'm having this much trouble thinking up things to talk about to a girl. For goodness sake, say something.

"Sometimes, I have trouble eating the food here too. You never know what's in there some days."

She doesn't smile or react in any way. I'm striking out here. I need to change the subject.

"Where're you from?"

"Philly," she replied. "Germantown area."

I smiled at her and gave some lame comment. *Ask something meaningful.*

"Did you just move here then?"

Instead of telling me to shove off for my lame question and answer session, she actually responded and even asked me a question.

It's small talk, but I'm ecstatic that she's actually conversing with me. I need to act fast before she loses interest.

I tripped over my words, but I managed to ask her out to an upcoming party. However, Sara immediately hugged herself, as if she were trying to protect herself from me. *I moved too fast and now she's pulling away. What could have her so wound up? I wish I could read her mind.*

"I can't," replied Sara.

That stung, although I figured she would say no after I noted her reaction to my question. It seemed she had more to say about my invitation, but stopped herself short. I decided to make light of her refusal. *I can always ask her later.*

"Oh, that's too bad. Maybe some other time."

Good, she didn't grimace at that suggestion.

At least, I hoped Sara would give me another chance to take her out. My hope wavered when she shrugged. Either I've messed up, or she's got other things on her mind. For sanity's sake, I held on to the latter thought. I finished my lunch without saying anything else. I didn't want to push her further away. She wasn't eating much and it suddenly dawned on me I had not seen her smile at all. I began thinking she just doesn't want to be here.

"There's the bell. We better go. Class starts in five minutes. I can take your tray if you want," I offered.

"No, thanks. I got it."

I picked up my tray and followed her out the cafeteria door. At a loss for what to say, I walked next to Sara in silence to our next class. As it turned out, we're in Spanish class together, too.

When Spanish ended, she rushed out before I could get to her. *I'll try again tomorrow. Perhaps, it was an off day for her. At least, I hope so.*

I finished out my day and briefly met with Taylor before heading for my car. I caught a glimpse of Sara as she got on her bus. *I wonder where she lives.* On a whim, I decided to follow her bus. I discovered she lived a few streets from my house which made me smile. I kept driving so she didn't notice me. *The last thing I need is for her to think of me as a stalker. Mom will want to know how my day went, but I think I'll keep Sara a secret a little while longer. I would hate for her to fuss over me if things with Sara don't quite work out.*

GREAT PAINS TO BUILD A FRIENDSHIP
ଓ

I saw Sara get off the bus. I wanted to approach her, but after yesterday, I knew I'd better take it slow. Our class schedule was different today. I didn't get to see her much during the morning. I'll make a point of seeing her at lunch. Maybe, I'll luck out by talking to her about my interest in music.

I walked up to Sara's table which didn't seem to cause her as much discomfort as it did yesterday.

"Hi, Sara. How's it going?" I asked, taking a seat without asking permission this time.

"Ok, I guess. What about you?" Sara responded quietly.

Wow, I never expected her to ask me anything. This seems promising.

"Pretty good, actually. I think it's going to be a good year."

I paused briefly trying to figure out how to tell her what I wanted to say.

"I don't know if you like playing musical instruments but the music room is open after school for anyone who wants to practice. I plan on going there Mondays, Wednesdays, and Fridays."

Her eyes brightened for the first time. Jackpot.

"I love playing piano. My dad started to teach me violin, but I'm not very good."

"Really, your dad plays? That's cool. Maybe I can hear him sometime."

Sara became sad again, and I played my response over in my head, trying to figure out what I said wrong.

"My dad's not alive anymore."

"Oh, sorry. When you said your parents moved here, I thought," I said, trying to redeem myself.

"It's my fault. I wasn't clear. My mom remarried."

"I hope you don't mind me asking, but how did he die?"

"He was playing in a bar one night when it was robbed. He got caught in the crossfire."

"I'm so sorry, Sara."

"Me too."

I didn't want to change the topic too quickly, but I hated seeing her sad again.

"Do you still play?"

"No, but I really miss it."

"I could teach you where your dad left off, if you like. I'm good at it. Do you have a violin?"

"Not any more. My step-father has no interest in musical instruments, so he sold my violin when he moved in."

"That's ok. I think there's an extra one in the music room. I think you can get permission from the music teacher to take it home sometimes."

"I can't, but thanks for telling me."

Sara hugged herself again and stared at her tray. I didn't know what to say, so I did the most sensible thing I knew how. I decided to leave her alone.

"I better go. I'll see you in class."

I grabbed my tray when I heard her gasp.

"Stay," Sara said weakly, moving one hand so its palm faced me. "Please," she continued, her voice shaken.

I immediately sat down.

"Ok, I'll stay. Is there something you wanted to talk about?"

She shook her head indicating she had nothing in particular to say. It seemed she just didn't want to be alone. I took a bite of my lunch, swallowed, and thought I would ask her about her background.

"You know, I've been wondering where you come from…I mean, your family. You have neat features, but I can't seem to place the origins."

"My mother is a full-blooded Italian from South Philadelphia. My father was African-American and German."

"Do you have brothers and sisters?" I asked.

"Yes, three, all younger. My brother Dontae is twelve, my sister Elena is eleven, and another brother Joel is five. Your turn," she said with confidence.

She started to relax around me and even took a bite or two of her lunch.

"My mother is Hispanic and American Indian. My dad was Japanese and African-American. He was killed during a tour to the Middle East. I'm an only child."

"That explains the shape of your eyes."

I thought she almost smiled. It was as if she tried to remember how and decided to give up trying. In the next second, the sadness came back.

"What's wrong, Sara?"

Her eyes appeared to plead for understanding. I was ready to forgive whatever it was she thought she did badly.

"I was abrupt yesterday when you asked me to the party this weekend. I am grateful you asked, but I feel like I should explain…"

Just then, Taylor rushed up to the table and started blabbing about football, the coach, and the cheerleaders. No "excuse me". No "who's your friend?" Before I could scold him for being so inconsiderate, Sara took her tray and slipped away.

I glared at him for a few seconds before he realized I was furious. "Wha'?" asked Taylor, clueless.

"That was so rude, Tay. You chased her off."

"She'll get over it. Everyone else does. Is she coming to the party? I'll apologize there."

"No, and she was just about to tell me why when you interrupted her. Sometimes, you can be a real moron."

I got my tray and started off after Sara, but I didn't see her anywhere. I felt we were really getting somewhere, that she started to trust me. Now, I don't know if she'll ever be this relaxed again.

I hoped she would show up in one or both of the last two classes of the day, but she wasn't there. As I promised myself, I went to the music room to play some piano. I wished against hope that she would show up, but again no Sara.

That evening after school, I stopped at Aunt Emma's house to get her input. Her job as a social worker brings her into contact with people who have lots of emotional problems. I thought she might be able to help me reach out to Sara.

After catching Aunt Emma up on all the details, she thought about how to answer.

"Well, Rick, it seems that your friend Sara is exhibiting self-preservation behavior, but it also seems like you've gained some of her trust. If something huge is going on in her life, it may take time for her to confide in you. All I can suggest is to be very patient. Music may be an escape for her since it brightened her disposition, but remember not to force her to do anything. You may lose her then."

"So, do I just keep trying to be her friend?"

"Yes, learn more about her so you can figure out what she needs. When she's comfortable, she'll tell you more."

"I think she wanted to tell me something today, but Taylor cut her off. I was so ticked off at him."

"Well, you may want to bring that up with her eventually, but wait until she's ready."

"Ok. Thanks, Aunt Emma. See you later."

"Ok, Rick. Bye, and let me know if you need to talk some more about this. You don't have to do this alone."

When I got home, I made dinner because Mom had to work a few extra hours at the hospital. She loved working as a nurse, but sometimes she had to work crazy hours which meant I had no one else at home to talk to.

When I finished eating, I started on my homework. I thought about Sara for the rest of the night. I could swear I even dreamt about her, but all I remembered were blurred images and choppy conversations.

I looked forward to seeing her in homeroom the next morning, so I could apologize to her. However, when I got to school, the principal called an emergency assembly in the auditorium, so I never got the chance to connect with her.

In addition, she did a great job avoiding me in every class we had together that day. Even at lunch, when I finally caught up with her, she appeared aloof. I tried to apologize for Taylor's behavior, but beyond a brief "that's ok", she did not speak another word. I started feeling all my progress had taken a step into the abyss of distant emotions.

After school, I would have headed home, but something drew me to the music room. I guess I thought I would play something. Playing the piano always had a way of relaxing me when I got worked up about something.

To my surprise, I heard music coming from the piano in the room. I wasn't familiar with that piece. In fact, it almost sounded original. When I got close enough to look inside, I found Sara playing. I had no idea she would even come here. Nothing in her actions gave me any indication she would pursue my indirect suggestion.

But, Sara was here, playing the most beautiful modern piece I had heard in a while. When she finished, I stepped into the room.

"Sara, that's beautiful, what's it called?"

Immediately, she stiffened and swung around to look at me in horror.

"Sorry, I didn't mean to startle you," I apologized.

"It's not you. I'm late for my bus. I have to run," Sara rattled off.

There were no sheets of music. What she played, she played from memory. But who taught her this song? Her dad perhaps? But something scared her. What was she thinking about?

I left the room puzzling over tons of thoughts rushing around in my head. *Maybe, she'll be willing to answer my questions tomorrow.*

HEALING THROUGH SONG
ᔭ

I'm not sure why I cried last night. Perhaps, I'm working too hard trying to please other people like my step-father or my mother. I hardly exist anymore and I surely don't exist to have pleasures that make me happy – like music.

I miss playing the piano. I wish I could play the violin.

I wish I could go to that party Rick told me about and meet the other kids. I wish...

My mom kissed me goodbye for my second day of school, and I noticed the black and blue circles around her left eye. Chuck had hit her again.

She pushed me gently out the door and wished me well. I felt like crying for her, but I choked back the tears.

I was relieved to find that Rick wasn't in any of my morning classes. I needed some time to decide what I wanted to do about him. Whatever that turned out to be, my deepest desire drew my mind to the same conclusion – I wanted him to be my friend.

Rick stopped by my table during lunch and sat across from me as though we had been long time friends. I liked that. It relaxed me.

At first, we made small talk, and then he brought up my favorite topic in the world – music. The words flew off my tongue as I told him about my musical interests in piano and the violin. But I made a mistake. I talked about my dad.

Talking about my dad could lead down many roads, none of which would have a happy ending. To talk about my dad meant I had to talk about his death. To talk about his death meant I had to talk about my step-father. To talk about my step-father meant I couldn't have friends. *I need to explain why I can't go to the party without really saying why.*

So, Rick asked me about my father, and I explained that Dad died. Then something amazing happened. Rick took a sour conversation and turned it around into a caring, heartfelt one. He seemed to genuinely care about me, about my feelings. Gosh, he's so easy to talk to. I found that I had become relaxed.

Then Rick said, "I could teach you where your dad left off, if you like. I'm good at it. Do you have a violin?"

Gosh, could you? At least that's what I wanted to say, but I knew I couldn't. I needed to start pushing him away. I needed to remain unhappy. Nothing I said derailed him. Rick had a solution for every problem I presented. I felt trapped by his goodness, so I hugged myself. That chased him away, but I couldn't bear to see him leave.

I asked him to stay.

Did I actually say that? I think my hand moved.

Rick looked confused.

"Please," I begged.

What am I doing? Am I crazy? This makes it even harder for me to let him go, for him to let me go. Why am I doing this? For the first time in my life, a stranger cares about me, and is more willing to walk away than to force me to do what he wants me to do. I need Rick in my life. I need him to stay.

Rick sat again, but I didn't know what to talk about. He said something positive about my features which surprised me. I always thought my main flaw, the freckles, would mask any possible beauty on my face. When I look in a mirror, the term 'neat features' does not readily come to mind, yet he is taken with me and it makes me feel good inside.

We continued to talk about our roots and our families. His father is dead too, but all I could concentrate on was the shape of his eyes. I felt almost dreamy. How insensitive of me!

The thought of this made me frown, not to mention the guilt I felt about having to explain why I couldn't go with him to the party.

"What's wrong, Sara?" Rick said tenderly.

My heart melted.

"I was abrupt yesterday when you asked me to the party this weekend. I am grateful you asked, but I feel like I should explain..." I started to say, but one of his friends interrupted me.

Perhaps, I shouldn't be saying any of this. I felt like running and did just that. I got my tray and, without saying goodbye, fled the cafeteria. I felt tears flowing down my cheeks. I couldn't let Rick see me like this. I would have to explain too much.

I was afraid that I would see Rick in my afternoon classes, but he wasn't in either one. I remembered him saying that he planned on practicing today, so I walked over to the music room not knowing what I would do or even if I would let him know I was there. I stood in the doorway watching him silently, but I walked away without him knowing. I couldn't face him, at least not yet.

On the way home, I sat on the bus next to the only Goth I encountered at school. No one else wanted to sit next to her, so she had become my daily bus companion. Today, she looked at me suspiciously. I wished I could tell what she thought, but perhaps I was better off not knowing.

That night, I stayed in my room while I finished my homework. It remained quiet. Chuck had to work the night shift at his security job. Imagine, a security job! Who would protect us from him at home?

When I got up the next morning, I wondered how I would avoid Rick. An emergency assembly made it easy. For my other classes, all I had to do was be the last one in and the first one out.

Lunch proved to be a problem. I could skip it, but considering it was the best meal I would eat all day, that wouldn't be such a good idea.

Needless to say, Rick caught up with me and started to apologize for the interruption the previous day. He had it all wrong. I should be the one apologizing for not being truthful, but I couldn't be sure I could trust him just yet. I didn't say anything beyond two words to him. I could tell it hurt him that I turned cold. I hated what I put him through. He looked lost, not sure how to reach me. *I'm not sure how to reach myself. Oh, Rick, I'm not worth getting to know. I'm damaged.*

I lasted through my remaining two classes and headed down to the music room. It's Thursday, so Rick shouldn't be there. I sat down at the piano and began playing the last song Dad wrote before he got shot. I loved the song. It reminded me of a lullaby with a slight rock edge.

When I finished playing, Rick said something to me. I can't remember what he said. The fact he stood there shocked me, causing my adrenaline to go into top gear. I had to get away from him. I had to get out.

"Sorry, I didn't mean to startle you," he apologized.

I heard what he said that time.

"It's not you. I'm late for my bus. I have to run," I said quickly.

I dashed down the hallway before he had the chance to stop me. *I don't know that I could resist if he did. I can't let him pursue me. If I do and Chuck finds out, my "introduction into womanhood" will be brutal. I'm afraid.*

My Goth bus buddy stared at me as I floundered with the strap on my bag, but she didn't say a word.

CLEARING THE AIR WITH SONG
&

Rick courageously joined me at lunchtime. He looked unsure of how to begin, so I made it easy for him.

"Rick, I'm sorry about yesterday. I wasn't ready to talk."

He looked at me intently for a few seconds before speaking.

"What was that song you played? It was well written."

Rick totally avoided any number of questions he could have asked. He went right to the topic that makes me relax the most.

"It was written by my father. He taught me how to play it a week before he died. It's my favorite of all his original pieces."

Rick shuffled in his seat and looked toward his friends.

"Rick?"

He looked at me.

"I never finished what I started to say two days ago."

He waited patiently. He didn't move. I could hear him breathing.

"I…I wanted to let you know that I wished I could go to the party, but I can't. I'm not allowed," I said in barely more than a whisper. I felt I might hyperventilate.

"Oh, if your parents are worried about us going together, I can make other arrangements. I just wanted you to meet some people."

"That's just it. I'm not allowed to hang out with other kids. It's not just because you asked me out."

"What? That's crazy. Why, Sara?"

"It's complicated. I'm sorry."

I wanted to say more.

"Don't be. We can still be friends, right?" he asked, seemingly resolved and hopeful.

I felt my eyes starting to water.

"I need to go, Rick. I'm sorry."

"Sara."

The sound of my name from his lips reminded me of a parent cradling a new born baby. He was careful with it, gentle, almost protective. That sound resonated in my brain as I walked out of the cafeteria toward my next class.

I tried to convince myself that I was doing the right thing. I fought to stay away, but after the final bell rang, I found myself walking toward the music room, toward Rick. He looked so hurt in Spanish.

I don't want to be the cause of his pain.

I heard him playing the treble clef of *Linus and Lucy*. *I want him to be my friend, to rescue me from my life!*

It sounded somber, seeming to represent his mood. I walked quietly into the room, dropped my bag, and slid onto the bench next to him. He stopped playing.

I slid closer to Rick to get positioned to play the bass clef of the piece. My nerves racked sitting so close to him, but I fought the urge to leave.

I placed my left hand on the keys and started to play. Rick joined in and we played the song as if we were one. It felt glorious like this was meant to be.

After we finished the piece, I felt a shiver. I hoped he didn't notice.

"I want to be your friend so much, but my step-father has forbidden me to make friends with anyone." I couldn't look at him.

"Then, it'll be our secret, Sara. I don't want to get you in trouble, but I do want to be your friend," Rick said, trying to reassure me as he placed his hand over mine and held it firmly.

My heart fluttered and I pulled my hand away while slowly getting up.

"I should go now. I have to get to my bus."

"Sara, I'm sorry. I shouldn't have done that. Please don't run off," Rick begged.

I turned around, grabbed my bag, and flew out the door. I ran all the way to the bus. The driver was about to close the door when I arrived. Fear gripped my heart as I thought what would happen to me if I missed my ride home.

After taking my seat, I saw Rick at the front of the school panting.

My Goth bus buddy said her first words to me.

"It's none of my business, but it seems to me that he likes you. For that matter, I would bet you like him too."

Her words shocked me, not because they weren't true, but because the one person I thought didn't care, managed to notice the important details. Who else noticed?

"I can't do this. My parents…"

"Well, sweetheart, you need to make a choice, and you need to think about what you want in the end. Chances like this may only come around once in a lifetime. From what I know about him, he's a good kid."

She said nothing more for the rest of the ride, but I knew she had a point.

HOPE EXPOSED
෪

I touched Sara's hand. That's all I did. Why did she run? I thought for sure after we played so well together, she had finally relaxed with me. Instead, she seemed unsure at first, unsure of how to respond. What's wrong with her? Shouldn't she trust me by now that I just want to be her friend?

No…I'm still a stranger to her, and I still don't know what her baggage is.

Why would she think I'm different from any other guy? I moved too fast. I should never have touched her. I should have waited until she said it was alright.

I took off after Sara hoping to catch up and get to the bottom of her odd behavior, but she caught her bus in time. My chest hurt from the sprint, so I bent over trying to catch my breath. I wanted her to see that I could be a good friend, maybe more.

After Sara's bus disappeared down the street, I walked back to the music room to get my stuff. My feet dragged down the hallway. I pulled at my hair. I wished so much that I could talk to her right now.

I can't even call her to tell her I messed up.

૪૭

I went to the party that night, still perplexed over Sara's reaction. The speakers pumped out music that wafted around my body, drowning me in a fog. I stared at all the students who were dancing and laughing the night away.

"What's up, Rick?" asked Taylor.

"I'm not sure, Tay. Some things don't make sense."

"Are you talking about that girl I saw you talking to at lunch?"

I didn't want to talk about Sara. She might freak if other students started noticing her.

"It's nothing you need to worry about. I think I'll go home. I'll catch you later."

"Are you sure, Rick? It's not that late."

"Yeah, see ya."

The truth is I really wished I could talk to Tay about Sara, but sometimes he threw his tact on the ground. I just didn't want to cause Sara any more heartache. Maybe, someday soon I'll feel alright talking to him about her, but not tonight.

Monday morning, I waited in my car until Sara's bus arrived. Grabbing my bag, I followed Sara to her locker. She was swapping books when I stopped next to her. *Are those red hi-lights in her hair? Focus.*

"Hi, Sara."

Her body did not turn rigid this time, but instead of looking at me, she cast her eyes toward the bottom of her locker.

"I'm really sorry I offended you. It's just that, well, it was fun, Sara. It seemed like we had always played music together. I didn't mean to make you run off."

I frustrated myself trying to find the right words.

"I guess what I really want to say is that I care. That's all I meant by holding your hand."

I waited. She shook her head and a strand of hair fell onto her temple.

"You didn't do anything wrong," Sara said, her voice so soft. "You're not the reason I ran away. Well...you are, but it's not your fault."

She looked at me then, her green eyes piercing mine.

"I thought all weekend about what you said, Rick. I *will* be your friend. I'm afraid, but I will be your friend."

I nodded. "So, we can still have lunch together?"

"I'd like that very much," admitted Sara.

I smiled, but she just closed her locker and walked next to me on the way to class.

A BREAK IN THE MADNESS
&

I didn't want him to feel guilty. He did nothing wrong. That's why I fought against everything inside me, pushing me to look away, when I looked into his eyes.

I try never to look someone in the eye – too intimidating. I would look at their mouth, my feet, to one side or the other, but never in the eye. I hear the eye is the window to someone's soul, but mine is too dark for someone as sweet as Rick to look into.

I dared take the risk because I refused to see Rick suffer for my sin, *my dirt*. Why does he even want to be my friend? If he knew what I've done, he might have different thoughts.

For the last three weeks, Rick and I have met after school to practice for his recital. He's even given me violin lessons so that I can join him on a few songs.

It was awkward at first, learning the violin from Rick. The first time he taught me how to position the bow, his hand shivered as it held mine. I felt no fear while I hung out with him. The music we played together made it easy for me to be near him.

Each lesson was short because I only had a few minutes before having to run to catch the bus. I surprised Rick with how much I remembered from day to day, but it has always been that way for me. Music holds me together. It's the only thing of value in my messed up life.

Yesterday, as I sat next to Rick on the piano bench, something strange started to happen between us.

"I'm really glad we've been able to do this. I like hanging out with you. You're a beautiful person," Rick said gently.

"Why do you say such things? I'm a nobody here," I responded, shaking my head.

"Not to me, Sara," Rick disagreed. "Not to me. You're beautiful inside, but you're beautiful on the outside too."

Slowly, Rick raised his hand and touched my cheek. I shivered then, and my heart began to race in my chest. He leaned toward me, but I grabbed his hand and removed it, backing away.

"I can't do this. This can't happen. It's time for me to go," I said, trying to ignore the somersaults my stomach experienced.

"Sara, please don't run off. We've talked about so many things. I feel I know you pretty well. I want to get closer."

He tried to touch my face again, but I backed away until I reached the door.

"You don't know me, Rick. There are things I can't tell you, not now, maybe not ever. I'm sorry," I said, grabbing my bag.

After taking in the dejected look on his face, I turned toward the hallway and ran away...again. My whole body ached from sorrow.

Rick was not far off the point. He knew a lot about me. We talked about my siblings and things we did for fun. *That* was a short conversation. We talked about the schools I attended and my favorite subjects. However, whenever he asked about my step-father, I quickly changed the subject by saying "I don't want to talk about him right now."

Rick never pushed me. Always backing off from the difficult topics, he waited patiently for me to take the conversation where I was most comfortable.

When I woke up the following morning, I felt like staying home. I didn't want to face Rick today. Don't get me wrong. I want the friendship. I think I need it right now, but if I mess up, if my step-father finds out about him, my life will be over.

Rick is the only sane thing I have right now. I don't want to mess things up with him. I'm getting up and going to school. It's Wednesday, so I won't see him until lunch time. How will I explain yesterday?

When I arrived at my table, Rick was already seated and half-finished with his lunch.

"I wanted to make sure I didn't miss you today. I hoped you wouldn't avoid me like you did last time," said Rick.

"No, I wouldn't do that to you again," I said, taking my seat. "I couldn't bear to see you hurt. I'm a mess and I'm sorry."

"No, Sara, you're not a mess. It's ok if you're not ready. I can wait until you are."

"About that, I want to try again. Will you be practicing today?"

"Are you sure about this? 'Cuz…'"

"Yes, I'm sure. Will you be there?"

"Yes," he replied, somewhat unsure.

I felt unsure too, but I knew I needed to take a chance. *My heart aches too much when I think about doing anything else.*

When I showed up in the music room after my last class, Rick was already there sitting on the piano bench, playing a piece for his upcoming recital. I walked up to the bench and sat. He looked at me and smiled.

"Are you ready?"

"I'm afraid," I admitted.

"It'll be ok," Rick assured me, and slid closer.

"I don't know about this," I said, sliding slightly away.

"I just want to kiss you."

"My step-father."

"He won't find out about this. You're safe." Rick paused briefly. "Do you want to do this?"

"Yes, very much." I couldn't believe I was saying those words. I can't believe I'm letting him in. "Can I trust you?"

"Yes," Rick answered, sliding toward me until our bodies pressed together.

Then Rick kissed me, before I had the chance to delay further. His lips felt soft. His hand cradled my cheek, and my hand held his, this time, in place. The warmth of his palm against my cheek felt comforting. I had forgotten what it was like to be touched and not have that touch be a slap against my face or a fist against my body, not to mention the harsh grabbing.

With Rick, I felt so many sensations, but the ones that stood out to me were my beating heart in an extremely relaxed body, and the feeling of safety.

When we stopped kissing, he looked at me and smiled as he bit on his lower lip. I leaned my head on his shoulder, burying my face in his neck. I didn't want to move from his arms now wrapped around me.

"I like you, Sara."

"I like you too, Rick."

He kissed me again.

"You're so beautiful."

"You don't know everything about me. You'd probably feel differently."

"I doubt that whatever you tell me will change how I see you, but I still want to know you better. You know you can tell me anything."

"Not here. Can we meet somewhere near our homes?"

"I'll try to find someplace."

"Ok. I should go now, or I'll miss my bus."

"I can take you home."

"No, my step-father watches the bus every day. If I'm not on it, I'll be in trouble."

Rick furrowed his eyebrows.

"Ok. See you tomorrow."

I made it to the bus in time, still in a daze from my close encounter. I sat down thinking about my first kiss, running my fingers along the place his lips touched.

"So it finally happened," said my Goth friend.

I consider her my friend because she seems to know so much about me. I've got to be more careful. I still don't know who I can truly trust.

THE HORROR CONTINUES
ဆ

That night, I slept all night for the first time – no nightmares. I woke up refreshed the next morning longing to see him. When I finally made it to homeroom, I sought out his face, the face that calmed my very soul. His eyes twinkled as he looked at me. I think I almost remembered how to smile.

I walked up to my desk and found a surprise – a pink carnation and a note. It smelled sweet and looked beautiful. They last a long time – carnations. If only I was as hardy as this flower. If only I were as beautiful.

I unfolded the note and looked at Rick before I read it. He looked away to give me a chance to focus on his note.

Oh, Sara, there are no words to describe how I felt yesterday. I care about you a lot and want to know you better. I know you're afraid, but I'll take care of you. I'll watch out for you. Don't hesitate to let me in.

Tears found their way to the rim of my lids. I wiped them away before they fell over the brim. I looked at Rick again. What have I done?

ଔ

We met at lunch and Rick frowned at me, but not the kind where he's sad. It was the kind where he's asking, "What's the matter?"

"Sara, why don't you smile? I mean, you seem happy with and relaxed around me playing instruments, but I don't see you smile. What's got you so bogged down?"

I wanted to tell him then and there, but I couldn't.

"Can I tell you when we meet outside school?"

He watched me carefully before saying, "Sure." Then he continued, "You know, I haven't been totally straight with you."

I looked at him curiously. What could *he* have to hide? Rick was always happy, well, except when I made him sad.

"What is it?" I asked, pulling my hand away.

Over the past few weeks, we worked our way up to touching finger tips while in the presence of staring eyes. I remained afraid to allow full-fledged hand holding in public. I did not want others to know how strongly I felt about him. I played with my braid using one hand and hugged myself with the other.

"Yesterday, I told you I liked you. Well, the truth is, I love you, Sara. I care for you very much and I was wondering if I could consider you my girlfriend."

I gasped. It's what I wanted, but I knew if I indulged, I could lose him forever.

"Oh, um, Rick," I stumbled. "I care about you too…" I couldn't say 'love' – too much…showing my true feelings without him knowing the truth about my life. "…but I need to tell you my secret first. Do you mind waiting until after we talk for my answer?"

He reached for my hand holding the braid and put it back on the table so he could caress my fingers.

"Nothing's gonna change how I feel about you. I'd be worried if you had a habit of killing your boyfriends, but I'd still love you. Short of that, I'd still talk to you and I doubt you'd hurt anyone."

I tried to say something, but no words came to mind. I'm not sure how I felt about his words.

"Sara, will you be at practice today?"

"Yes, I'll be there. I want to play something for you on the violin. I hope it'll sound ok."

"I look forward to it. By the way, my aunt said it was ok to meet in her shed on Saturday. I'll give you the address after school."

I couldn't wait to see Rick. As soon as the last bell rang, I rushed down the hallway. I didn't have to stop at my locker – my flower and note were securely hidden in my bag. Also, I learned to pack the books I needed for homework and the ones for my final two classes. That way, I could spend as much time as possible in the music room before having to catch the bus.

I found Rick smiling as he looked me over, eyes twinkling. Spontaneously, I unwrapped my arms and held them out to him. He hesitated, trying to make sure he understood my gesture. Rick opened his arms in response to let me slip between them, enabling me to rest my head on his shoulders. Relief ran through my body. I felt at home with him, safe at home.

"I've been working through some notes in my head, trying to imagine how I would play them on the violin. I don't know how it'll sound, but I wanted to try it. If it's bad, be honest."

"You bet," agreed Rick.

I believed him. He never tried to be mean, but he never shrunk back from telling me how I could improve my skills. Without instruments at home, improving anything became near impossible, but the five to ten minutes I spent practicing at school every day helped just the same.

I released him and grabbed the violin and bow. Taking a deep breath, I started to play *Twinkle, Twinkle Little Star*. Rick closed his eyes and listened intently. I messed up a few notes, but overall, I didn't think it was too bad. When I finished, I waited for his response.

Rick slowly opened his eyes and nodded.

"That was great, Sara. You had a few misses, but overall, your interpretation was fantastic. When did you practice this song?"

"I practiced the few days you couldn't stay after school. Besides that, I heard it in my head."

"You amaze me, Sara. It's almost like you're a prodigy. If you had access to instruments everyday for a few hours, you would easily pass me. I could never play like this with as little time as you've had."

Taking the violin and bow out of my hands, Rick replaced them in the case. Then, he looked at me. I tried to read his eyes when I felt his fingertips stroke my cheek seconds before he kissed me.

I was lost in the pleasure of it. Nothing else mattered at that moment, not school, not music, not...

My heart raced and I opened my eyes to look at the clock. My stomach heaved and I thought I would throw up.

"Oh, no. My bus," I yelled, pushing him away. "I can't miss my bus."

"It's ok, Sara. I'll take you home. Maybe I can get you there when the bus pulls up."

"You don't understand. He watches me walk off the stupid thing," I said breathlessly, immediately running down the hall and out the front door.

Once outside, I nearly fell flat on my face when a mental fog temporarily blocked all reason.

My bus was gone.

I felt like screaming, but the sound wouldn't come. I had to run, run fast and get home. Maybe he won't be there. Maybe he'll be busy raking the leaves.

"Oh, God, please don't let him notice I'm not on the bus."

I breathed deeply as my heart pumped faster. I decided to run the equivalent of ten zigzagged blocks home. My feet stumbled twice along the way, but I pressed on. I saw the bus once, crossing a path I had yet to reach. Waving, I realized the bus driver didn't see me. Liquid fell down my cheeks, and it seemed as if I looked through a glaze.

When I finally arrived home, I saw my bus bouncing down the street in the great distance ahead. I turned to look at my house and gulped hard as two blue eyes glared back at me. Sweat ran down my face, and my chest heaved from lack of air. Although my feet stepped onto the pavement to cross the street, my brain screamed at me to continue running down the street.

The urge to throw up increased when Chuck stood only ten feet away. I could see the sweat on his red face now and his fists, clenched tight. I kept walking toward him, my body now shaking intermittently.

Chuck's fists started to release. My throat went dry, trying to squeeze the life out of me before he had the chance. I had trouble breathing.

Chuck grabbed my braid and started yelling curses at me. My hand rose to my defense, fighting to keep my braid attached to my head.

"I'm sorry. I'm sorry. It won't happen again. Please don't. I promise…" I begged, but my knees gave way, and he dragged me into the house.

My bag fell off me just inside the door and I heard it slam shut. I heard screams from my siblings amid my hysterical gasping.

"Go hide," I begged them through a rasp sounding voice.

Three pairs of feet ran toward my room as Chuck dragged me to his. Mom grabbed his arm.

"You said you would wait! Please don't hurt her, not today!" screamed Mom right before he backhanded her against a cheek. She slammed against a doorpost and slid to the floor.

I reached out to her, but a slap along my chin made me jerk back.

Mom was sobbing now. "Take me. I'll take her place. Please. Her school…" begged Mom as she crawled toward us.

"Not this time. She has to pay for this herself. I won't take her today, but she will do what I want. Now get out unless you want to watch," he barked.

Mom backed out the door and closed it behind her. I could see her shadow just outside the door. She won't go far…just in case.

Chuck pulled his pants down and made me touch him, made me arouse him. He ordered me to use my mouth, but I shook my head. I hated that more than anything. I didn't want to. I felt a punch on my back as he threatened to hurt my sister. I did as he ordered.

Before he ejaculated, I pulled away, but quickly used my hands to finish the job. Sperm spilled to the ground, and I immediately got up, burst out of the room toward the bathroom and slammed the door. My stomach heaved three times before releasing the remaining contents of lunch that had not yet digested into the toilet.

I overheard Chuck yelling at Mom. She begged him to let her see me, but he threatened worse if she talked to me before he left for work. I didn't hear her voice anymore. I wasn't so sure I wanted her comfort. Her touch right now would seem an extension of him. I needed to get clean…at least on the outside.

I looked at myself in the mirror and hated the girl I saw. My hair, no longer in a braid, hung around my face. Strands clung to my cheeks where the sweat started to dry up.

"You're ugly," I said to the girl in the mirror. "Who could love you now? Who would want to kiss those used up lips?"

Banging my hand against the wall, I wailed at the top of my lungs. Love found me, but in one breath had lost me yet again.

I checked to see if I had locked the door. I didn't remember doing so, but it was locked. I ripped my clothes off and took a quick shower. Chuck hadn't raped me, at least what most people think of as rape, but I felt dirty all over. I scrubbed from head to toe, trying to get any traces of his scent off me. I scrubbed my lips until they hurt. Then, I slumped in the shower hugging myself, crying for a very long time.

I finally turned off the faucet and dried off. Slowly, I cracked open the door for any sign of Chuck, but I didn't see him. I only saw my mother curled up in one corner crying her eyes out. I knew she wished she could've switched places with me, but I didn't want to face her…not tonight.

I walked into my room hoping Dontae still hid in the closet with the younger kids, but there was no sign of them. This meant Chuck had left the house. Dontae would only leave my room if Chuck had left for work after an episode or dragged Dontae out for a beating. Since I didn't hear any yelling, I exhaled knowing Chuck had gone for the rest of the night. Hopefully, he won't be home before the bus arrived in the morning.

I stared at my body the next morning. Bruises could be seen the length of both arms where he grabbed me. My back still hurt from the punches I received each time I hesitated or refused. I got up to look at my face – not too bad. My chin grew red from the slap, but otherwise there were no bruises. I decided to wear a ponytail, but no braid. I needed to cover his hand print on my neck he created as he forced me to perform oral sex.

I had been raped alright. My dignity, my self-respect, my beauty, my peace of mind, and my innocence had been ripped from me over and over. Only numbness remained in their places. I thought there should be emotional pain. Perhaps that will come later. For now, the only pain I felt was physical.

Mom still slept when I left the house to catch the bus. I felt relieved. I really didn't want to talk to her this morning either.

It's Friday, so I won't see Rick until lunch. I don't know how I'm going to manage looking at him. He always seems to notice when I change my behavior. I hope he doesn't notice my bruises.

CONFESSIONS OF A BROKEN HEART
෮

I don't remember much from the morning. I don't recall eating breakfast, but I'm sure I did because I don't feel hungry. I'm sitting at a desk, so I must have gotten on the school bus. Everything sounds so far away, like an echo. The teacher asked me a question, but I didn't hear. I shook my head.

"Are you ill, Sara?" asked Mr. Johnson.

"I'm not quite myself today," I said, not wanting to lie, but knowing I couldn't tell the truth.

"Do you need to go to the nurse?"

"No," I said quickly. I couldn't afford the examinations. My family would be split up. "I think lunch will perk me up."

He accepted that answer, thank goodness.

I didn't think it was a lie. Rick's presence always brought out the best in me. I only wondered if he could rid the nasty film that had covered my soul.

It wasn't that cold out, so most kids still wore short sleeves. I looked extremely out of place wearing a sweater, but it was the only thing I could think of to cover all my bruises.

I sat at my special lunch table waiting for Rick. I didn't want him to see me like this, but if I avoided him today, I would surely lose myself.

I briefly thought of the flower and note Rick gave me yesterday. Chuck never knew I had them. My brother, Dontae, carried my bag to my room. After my shower, I hid the flower and note between the mattresses of my bed. I prayed there wouldn't be a reason for Chuck to tear apart my bedroom.

I saw Rick get his lunch and walk over to our table. I should be able to smile today after all the bonding we've experienced over the past few days, but that evasive smile would not come today. I'd be happy if I didn't break down in tears.

"Hey, Sara. Did you get home ok?" Rick asked, concern permeating his voice.

"I got home," I replied.

"What's wrong?" he asked, reaching out for my hand.

It's funny how well he reads me. He got a hold of my hand before I could pull it off the table and onto my lap. Because of my movements, he overextended his reach so I couldn't pull away. As a result, his hand brushed against the sleeve of my sweater, revealing the edge of the bruise on my wrist. *Did he see?*

"What's that, Sara?" Rick moved my sleeve to uncover a nasty black-n-blue bruise, and then he stared at me.

"I..." I didn't want to lie to him. "I hit my wrist against a doorway at home. Don't worry. It'll be fine."

Something in his face showed me he knew there was more behind my reply.

"Your step-father? Was he very upset?"

"How?" I wondered how he knew. I didn't remember seeing him outside after school. Could he have seen me running down the street?

"Some kids in my class told me they saw you running home. You missed your bus. I'm sorry."

"I don't want to talk about it right now, ok?" My chest ached.

He thought for a bit.

"I know I'll see you tomorrow, but I wanted to give you something and I don't have it on me. Would you stop by the music room this afternoon?"

"I can't miss my bus again."

"I promise not to keep you long."

"Ok, I'll be there."

My nerves were at a breaking point. I felt every pang that reminded me of the bruises all over my body from being slammed, slapped, and dragged.

I hugged myself as I entered the music room. I had reverted into my own space, not willing to let Rick in today. He frowned as he looked at me.

"I wanted to give you some music. I'll be playing my sax for this piece and I was hoping you could join me on piano," Rick said, extending his arm toward me.

I took the music and looked it over.

"I think I can do this. I'll study it this weekend. We can practice next week, ok?"

I started to turn away when he spoke again.

"Hey, wait. Don't I get a goodbye kiss? I missed you and I feel really bad about yesterday."

"I can't, not today."

"Sara," he said in earnest, grabbing my arm.

It wasn't a rough grab, but I winced at the pain it caused on my arm.

"Why did that hurt you? I didn't think I held you hard. How far up your arm does your bruise go?"

I couldn't speak. My brain jumbled all the words. The only thing my body remembered to do was produce tears. I fought to hold them back.

Rick pushed my sleeve up, further up than he did in the cafeteria.

"Gosh, Sara, what's going on here? I want to see. Can I see?"

I nodded feebly. I couldn't say 'no' to Rick. I wanted him to know me, even at the risk of him hating me like I hated myself.

Rick walked behind me and slid my sweater off my shoulders and down my arms. I wore a short sleeve dress, so he quickly saw the extent of the injuries on both arms. His fingers gingerly caressed my bruises as he gasped a few times.

Moving my ponytail, he examined my neck. I suppose he saw finger imprints because he spoke after pulling at my collar to take a better look at my back. I swallowed hard.

"Your step-father did this to you because you missed the bus?" Rick asked with a quivering voice.

I nodded again. I'd forgotten how to speak.

He replaced my sweater over my shoulders.

"Oh, God, why did he do this to you?"

I often asked God that question. It was strange hearing it from a voice not my own.

"Sara, it's my fault this happened to you. I'm so sorry."

His thumbs were busy wiping the tears from my cheeks, and I found my thumbs doing the same on his. I started taking in shallow breaths. I needed to leave. I couldn't relive the previous day.

"Rick, I must go now, but I'll tell you everything tomorrow. I can be there after lunch around one," I said, my voice quivering.

"I'll be waiting in my aunt's house. Here's the address I forgot to give you yesterday. When I see you, I'll come out to the shed. It'll be open."

He tried to kiss me, but I placed my fingers on his lips. I couldn't let him kiss me, not after what I had to do the day before. "I can't right now. I'll explain tomorrow. I promise."

His eyes exposed his hurt. Reluctantly, he released me, so I could leave him alone wondering if I would indeed show up at his aunt's shed. But, I'll be there, even if I crawl there taking my last breath.

&

I go for walks often around the neighborhood, so leaving today shouldn't seem out of place to Chuck. The only problem is the time. What else is new?

I usually walk for an hour. Whenever I pushed the limits of that invisible time limit, I would meet Chuck glowering at me on the sidewalk instead of working on the garden.

What's funny is that I don't spend time enjoying the garden he toils over day after day. Once, Elena got excited when she saw a butterfly flitting from flower to flower in July. I hadn't noticed the butterfly. What's worse, I never noticed the flowers blooming along the path leading to our house. I was a walking zombie when it came to beautiful things.

So, as zombie-like Sara, I walked down the street, turned right, and walked a few more blocks before checking I wasn't being followed. I turned left and passed a few houses before reaching Rick's Aunt Emma's house. With a car parked in the driveway, I knew someone was home. I walked around back and found the shed.

Pulling the door toward me, I stepped inside. It smelled like musty grass and gasoline. I looked for somewhere to sit and finally noticed the twin bed sized blanket spread out on the right side of the shed.

I hardly got settled when Rick pulled open the shed door and stepped inside. It was warm for a day in fall, so he wore a t-shirt which clung to the muscles on his arms and abdomen. My heart fluttered. He looked stronger and bigger than I remembered him at school. Perhaps, it's because I sat on the ground peering up at him. It didn't take him long before he sat near me on the blanket, holding my hand. He tried to hug me.

"I can't. My step-father smells my clothes. If I smell like someone else, I'll get into trouble."

Rick acquiesced and sat back on his heels.

"I don't have much time, maybe thirty minutes," I warned.

"Summarize everything, then. I want to understand what's happening to you. I'll try to sit quietly and listen," he said.

"After Daddy was killed, Mom tried to take care of us on her own. With his line of work as a musician, he didn't leave much for us to live on. Mom got food stamps to supplement her job, but it still wasn't enough to keep a steady roof over our heads.

"For almost two years, Mom got one job after the other and dragged us from apartment to apartment. I would look after my siblings while she worked, but neighbors didn't like the idea of a young teen taking care of three children under twelve.

"One day, she came home and said she met someone she liked. In two weeks, they were married. At first, he acted ok, a little rough on the edges, but ok. As days became weeks, he became more violent towards my mother. When he got tired of her, he came after me."

Rick winced when I talked about me. I could see he wanted to talk, but he shook his head and remained silent. I continued my story.

"At first, he would only make me lay next to him with only my underwear on, so he could fantasize about me. However, that quickly turned into something worse."

Rick got up, fists clenched, and paced the room. He unclenched his fists and ran both hands through his hair and pulled at the strands before returning to my side.

"I'm sorry. Continue," he said.

I waited briefly trying to interpret his contorted features.

"Um, he started making me…arouse him. He made me touch him with my fingers and my…" I couldn't finish the sentence, so I just pointed to my lips. Rick understood because he looked as if he would lose whatever he ate for breakfast.

"What?! I know I said I would try to be quiet, but are you saying he made you…it?"

I cringed at hearing him say the words I dared not say myself.

"Yes."

"What else is he making you do?"

"Nothing, yet," I answered his question trying to prevent my voice from shaking.

"Yet? When?"

"On my eighteenth birthday."

"Which is?"

"December 3rd."

He exhaled a quick breath.

"That's the night of my recital."

Rick thought for a second and then looked up at me.

"What happened two days ago when you missed the bus?"

My body shivered. I hung my head and stared at the blanket. I couldn't look at his face anymore, especially during the next few minutes.

"I ran outside and saw that my bus was already gone. I didn't know what else to do, so I ran all the way home. I kept seeing the bus, but it was always too far away. I was so tired when I got home.

"Chuck was furious and grabbed my hair. He dragged me into the house as I struggled. I thought it was over, that he wouldn't wait until my birthday. Mom begged him not to hurt me, reminded him of his intention to wait. She wanted to take my place. She always tries to, but sometimes he wants me too much. He refused her request to take my place, but said he wouldn't do more to me, at least not yet.

"I yelled at my siblings to hide. We always hide in my closet when Chuck rapes our mother. We cover our ears so we don't hear her screams. I didn't want them to hear me scream. I didn't want him to hurt them.

"I kept struggling. I think that's when I bruised my arms against the doorpost and later the bed frame. I did what he told me when he threatened to harm my little sister. I don't want to tell you the details." I looked at him, afraid he would want to hear more.

"You don't have to. I know what he made you do," Rick whispered as he stared blankly past me.

"Afterwards, I ran to the bathroom and threw up. I hate what he made me do."

I fell silent, wiping away the tears as they flowed down my face. I've never told this story to anyone before. The possibility of losing Rick scared me.

He looked at the blanket, talking to himself. His eyebrows furrowed and released a few times. My heart sank as it dawned on me what he must be struggling with – he can't bear to touch me now that he knows I'm soiled.

"It's ok," I began, "I understand that you can't be with me now. Thanks for trying to be my friend."

I started to get up, but my muscles were too weak. Rick reached out and touched my cheek. Oh, how I love his touch. It doesn't hurt, does me no harm.

"Sara, you got it all wrong. I still love you. I still want to be with you. What's happened to you is awful, and I feel...responsible...for what you went through two days ago. I'm hurting because I did this to you. The bruises, what he made you do, *my* fault."

"No, it's not. Don't blame yourself for giving me much more than I deserve, for loving something as soiled and ugly as I am."

"Don't say that, Sara. You're very beautiful. I understand, with all you've been through, if you can't see that or believe that, but it's true. You're attractive, you're bright, and have a great personality.

"I often wondered why you were so reserved. It all makes sense now. Now, I know why you don't smile."

"I thought I would remember how to smile after I told you the truth, but without you, I can't."

"Sara, I'm still here. I'm not running away from you. I love you, Sara," he reassured me.

"I don't know if I feel the same. I know I care for you a lot...but I don't know if I feel love. I don't know if I know what it's like to feel that for someone."

"It's ok. I know you feel close to me and I know you want to be near me. That's enough. Sara?"

"What is it, Rick?"

"We've got to get you out of that house, so he won't hurt you anymore."

"Rick, I know, but I can't risk not keeping my family together. Promise me that you won't do anything unless you can guarantee my siblings and mother stay with me. Otherwise, I couldn't be around you anymore."

Rick struggled with that thought, but he nodded.

"I'll do whatever it takes to make sure you stay together. I promise."

"I should go now. It feels like I've been here a long time."

I walked to the door, when Rick slipped his hand gently into mine.

"Wait, you never gave me an answer."

"An answer…to what?"

"Will you be my girlfriend?"

"You still want me after all I've told you?"

"Yes, why not?"

"Because…"

Rick leaned closer to kiss me, but I stopped him with my free hand.

"We probably shouldn't kiss. I don't think he's sick, but I don't want to get you sick if he is. Gosh, I probably gave you whatever he has already."

"Exactly, it's too late for that now. I'm not too worried about it, although I probably should be. Anyway, since I've got whatever you do, there's no sense in not kissing you, right?"

"I guess so."

"So the only question that remains is, do you want to kiss me, as my girlfriend?"

Rick cheated a little. He combined two questions into one, but it didn't matter. I knew I wanted to say 'yes' to both anyway.

"Yes, I want you to be my boyfriend and I want you to kiss me."

Without pulling me close – I guess he remembered about my step-father smelling my clothes – Rick kissed me gently. I felt his love with that kiss, more than the others before this one because he knew everything about me and still wanted me.

I backed away slowly.

"See you Monday."

Rick caressed my cheek and then let me go.

"See you Monday."

I closed the door behind me, leaving him inside the shed. As I walked toward the street, the world seemed to come alive with color around me. Mums of various bright colors lined the garden. There were purple cabbages too. Why didn't I notice these before? I saw a lot of things on the way home that I never saw before because someone loved me in spite of my soiled soul.

HOW TO HELP WITHOUT THE HURT
ಐ

God, I can't believe what I just heard!

I didn't leave the shed right away. I returned to the blanket and sat there dumbfounded for another thirty minutes. I racked my brain trying to figure out a way to help get Sara out of this situation, free her without jeopardizing the closeness she shares with her mom and siblings.

It's crazy that anyone has to experience such torture. She's just a kid like me, but understands fears and malice I never have experienced. What Sara has lived through totally explains why she's so withdrawn and hesitant about herself and making new friends. I guess it's amazing she let me in at all.

How am I going to help her?

So far, music has helped her get in touch with happier feelings. She'd almost relaxed enough a few times to smile, but the heartache she returns to at home seems to get in the way. Or, perhaps, it's the fact that she likes me that stops her. If her step-father ever found out about me…

Well, I can't let that happen. There's no way I want to be responsible for any more attacks against her.

I like hearing Sara play. She's amazing. It seems like her essence is tied to music somehow. I wish we could spend more time together doing what we both love the most.

I thought about the first time I tried to kiss her. Man, I didn't have a clue what I must have put her through. She spends so much time trying to escape being forced to do something she doesn't want to do, and then I come along and try to make her kiss me. No wonder she freaked out. I'm surprised she talked to me after that, especially after all the times I asked about her step-father. Man!

I'm surprised she wanted me to kiss her in spite of everything.

I remember feeling doubtful whether she really wanted to kiss me or if she was afraid of losing me if she didn't. I racked my brain trying to remember any sign, any clue she gave to let me know if she felt afraid of us being together, of me.

I fast-forwarded my memories to the day after she let me kiss her. Well, I did linger on the kissing part. It felt great to remember her smell, her touch. I remembered the first time she hugged me. Usually, Sara hugs herself, but she let go of her fears enough to let me into her heart. Now that I think about it…that was huge.

I can't believe that the best time we enjoyed together turned into a living nightmare for Sara because I felt drawn to her after she played a simple children's song. I kissed her, and she forgot to check the time.

The buses spend between fifteen and twenty minutes waiting to be boarded, but if you're late, it's a phone call to the parents or a long walk home.

Usually, Sara would sprint down the hallway after practice to make the bus. She's had a few close calls, but she always made it. This time she didn't.

Gosh, it felt so good to kiss her.

I'm so sorry, Sara, that I didn't get you out in time. I didn't realize…

I talked to Aunt Emma that night. Nothing made sense. I couldn't figure out why Sara's face turned pale when she realized she missed the bus.

(Sigh).

I also didn't understand Aunt Emma's expression when I told her what happened. I bet Aunt Emma had an idea about the cause of Sara's extreme behavior, but she didn't want to worry me.

It's strange, but I don't think Sara wanted me to worry about her either. It's almost like she tried so hard to keep me away from the horrors she braced herself for on a daily basis.

If I hadn't seen her bruises, I don't think she would have told me about them.

Man, I almost gagged when I saw the black and blue marks all over her arms and back. How could anyone do this to another human being, especially to one living in the same house?

I felt so responsible and scared. He could have killed her. Yet, she didn't blame me for any of it.

Instead, Sara felt guilty for kissing me. True, I am a little concerned about STDs, well, actually a lot concerned, but I don't regret kissing her. I hope her step-father didn't pass something to her, but if he did, I guess I'll – we'll – have to deal with it the best way we know how. Mom wouldn't like it one bit, though. She's always lecturing me about stuff like that.

I finally got up and folded the blanket. The time arrived to talk to my aunt, although I wasn't sure how I would say what I wanted to tell her. I walked through the back door of Aunt Emma's house where she busied herself making a fruit salad.

"Is everything alright, Rick?" she asked without looking up.

"Aunt Emma?"

"Spill it, Rick. I'm listening."

"Can I talk to you about a hypothetical situation?"

"Sure. Go on."

"Hypothetically speaking, if someone is being abused...let's say, sexually...at home, what would you do to help that person?"

"Well, if he or she was willing to get help, an intervention could be put in place with help from the police and social workers. A restraining order or a new residence are a couple options."

"What could be done for a whole family? Um, would they be kept together or would they have to split up?"

"It depends on the size of the family and the space available in any safe houses." She paused. "Er, Rick, this sounds serious. Does this have anything to do with the girl who met with you today?" Aunt Emma asked, now looking up at me.

I shifted my footing and looked out the window.

"Is she or someone else in her family being hurt?"

I looked at her again.

"If I answer your question, are you obligated to pursue this case?" I asked. I needed to make sure Sara's family wouldn't be split up. I didn't want to lose Sara, not now after all we've been through.

"Yes, Rick, of course. I couldn't sear my conscience like that. I would have to help."

"Then I can't tell you for sure. I can only talk to you of a hypothetical situation. If you think you can keep my hypothetical family intact, then perhaps I can share reality with you."

"Rick, please."

"Aunt Emma, I've tried never to lie to you, but Sara means a whole lot to me, and I need to know what you can or cannot do before I tell you anything else."

"Alright. Have you spoken to your mother?"

"Not yet, not about this."

"Talk to her first. Then, I'll call her and we'll see what we can do about your hypothetical family."

"Thanks, Auntie."

I kissed her on the cheek before grabbing the bag of fruit she held out to me and walking out the front door.

That evening, I had the unfortunate circumstance of talking to my mom about my hypothetical abuse victim and the possibility of sexually transmitted diseases. Mom glared at me for a moment before settling down and encouraging me to get tested when I felt comfortable enough to do so.

I struggled with bringing up Sara because I didn't want my mom to ask to see her. Who knows how that first introduction would go over? However, I knew I could trust my mother's judgment if not her vocal restraint.

She offered the same testing for Sara whenever and if she wanted to be sure. I didn't doubt Sara would want to check, if for no other reason than to reassure herself she didn't harm me in any way. However, getting her alone to be tested would be another problem altogether.

PANIC SETS IN
෨

Monday couldn't come fast enough. I saw Sara on Saturday, and all I could think about was how to set her free of that demon of a step-father.

But how was I supposed to do that and still keep her family together?

I waited in my car until her bus showed up. My heart felt lighter when I saw her walk off the bus onto the walkway heading up to the main door. I grabbed my bag and ran over to meet her.

"Good morning, Sara."

"Hi, Rick."

I think she almost smiled. Her full mouth curved up on one side just a bit.

"It's good to see you," I said.

"You too. I wasn't sure you'd want to see me after what I told you on Saturday."

"Are you kidding? I couldn't stop thinking about you. I spent the rest of the weekend trying to figure out how to see you before today."

Then, I saw it. Sara smiled at me. In fact, it was a grin. Her eyes glistened over.

"Thanks, Rick, thanks for still wanting to be near me."

I walked Sara to her locker before revealing the orange mum I picked for her from Mom's garden.

"I wish I could've gotten something better for you."

"It's fine. I like it."

Why did it have to be Monday? I don't get to see her until lunch. The morning classes couldn't go fast enough. Sara waited for me at our table when I finally exited the lunch line.

"What took you so long?"

"I had to talk to the teacher, something about a special project she wants me to do for class. How was it this morning?"

"The usual. Nothing exciting."

There was no graceful way of asking her about her reception at home, so I jumped right into it.

"Sara, was everything alright when you got home on Saturday?"

She looked up from her lunch with a detached gaze. Did I jump into it too quickly?

"Yeah. He glared at me when I got home, but he didn't approach me. I went inside and washed my clothes right away. Mom wanted me to do some of Chuck's laundry. I was going to object until I realized I could use that situation to my advantage."

"Great. I was worried about you."

We continued eating our lunch before I interrupted the silence.

"I was thinking we could do something different tomorrow."

"What's that?"

"How would you like to sit with some of our classmates over there?" I suggested, nodding in the direction of the table crowded with kids I got along with well enough.

"I don't know."

"It'll be fine."

"Rick, you know I'm not allowed to have friends."

"Yet, you broke that rule when you started hanging with me. Why not keep going? Why stop half-way? I doubt anyone here is going to tell your step-father you had lunch with them."

"Will they accept me?"

"Why not?"

Then she did it again. Sara wrapped her arms around her torso.

"They'll accept you well enough, but you'll need to work on something."

"What?"

"Do you realize you hug yourself a lot?"

"Um, sorry," she said, releasing her body.

"No, don't be sorry. I think I get why you do. Do you mind if I help you break the habit?"

"I guess..."

"So are you up to eating with them tomorrow?"

It took her a few seconds. Sara stared at her food while she thought over my proposition.

"I'll give it a go…for you."

I was happy she would try something different. Why did it bug me so much that she said it was for me?

After a few minutes, the bell rang marking the end of the lunch period. We grabbed our trays and headed for our lockers.

"Sara, will you stop by the music room today?"

"No, I can't today or tomorrow. I'll try to on Wednesday."

I sighed.

"I want to kiss you, Sara."

"Me too."

I felt elated.

"Come with me," I said, pulling her toward a nook in the wall for limited privacy.

"But…" Sara objected.

I knew she had reservations. I knew she didn't want to infect me with whatever, if anything, her step-father passed on to her.

"I went on the internet. We should be ok if we avoid sharing saliva," I assured her…and myself.

Sara quickly wiped her mouth with the back of her hand and I mimicked her actions. I kissed her, pressing my lips to hers. It went quickly, too quick, and I was left wanting more.

"I love you, Sara."

"I…" she began, but struggled in vain to continue.

I knew that although she had strong feelings for me, saying 'I love you' was challenging with everything going on at home.

"It's ok," I said. "I know you feel connected to me even though you can't say it."

I kissed her again before she could agonize over what she couldn't say to me. Then I led her back into the hallway so we could walk our separate ways.

I didn't want to let her go.

I knew I wouldn't see her until homeroom tomorrow. The music teacher wanted to see me after school to review my choices of pieces to perform on December third. I hoped I could at least walk Sara to the bus, but that won't be possible, not today.

ଔ

How I wish I could go out on a regular date with Sara. It's so crazy, all this hiding. I can't wait to see her today.

I grabbed a breakfast bar, kissed my mom, and dashed out the door to the car. Too many red lights are getting in my way today.

Sara's bus pulled away the moment I got to the parking lot. After breezing by a guy who gawked at a girl, I parked the car and rushed inside.

Sara was sitting and reading a book when I finally slid through the door to homeroom. She looked up and smiled at me. I walked over and knelt beside her desk.

"I missed you, Sara."

"I missed you too," she said softly.

I gave her a quick kiss on the cheek before skipping back to my desk.

ଔ

Sara seemed nervous as we walked to the crowded table. Twice, I encouraged her to keep moving when her feet stopped dead. Finally, we reached the table of laughing friends.

"You guys mind if we sit with you today?" I asked lightheartedly.

"Not at all. Grab a seat," answered Jan.

I motioned for Sara to sit across from me. Yeah, I had ulterior motives. I wanted a full view of her face and sitting next to her would make that difficult to accomplish.

At first, conversation went well. Everyone introduced themselves to Sara and she seemed to feel at ease. However, before long, Sara's arms slowly moved into place around her torso. She looked at me and I nodded toward her arms. Understanding my cryptic sign language, Sara unwrapped her arms. From that moment on, Sara became quiet.

"So, Rick," started Jan, "are you and Sara an item?"

The question took me off guard. Sara and I hadn't really discussed whether or not we would expose that little known fact about our relationship. But then I thought about the way I acted. It's not like I've been covertly expressing my love for Sara. No doubt someone saw the flowers, note, kiss, and thought the very thing Jan asked. I looked at Sara for some clue, but all I got was an unrevealing stare.

"Uh, yeah, Sara's my girlfriend."

Musical variations of "cool" flowed from the lips of all my friends sitting at the table. Sara seemed relieved.

After we finished eating, everyone said they were glad we joined them for lunch. Sara and I waved before leaving the cafeteria.

"Are you ok?" I asked when we stopped by Sara's locker.

"Yes, I'm good. Your friends are nice."

"But they still made you uncomfortable?"

"I'm sorry, Rick. I can't add anyone else to my life. Having you is as much of a risk I'm willing to take. I need time to add more people. Will you be angry if we just ate by ourselves for awhile longer?"

"No, Sara. I'm the one that should apologize. I pushed you too fast. I'm sorry too. Do you mind that I told them we're together?"

"No, I'm glad you did," Sara said before looking at me.

I melted. The next thing I remember is my lips touching hers. When I came to, I realized the bell had rung, making me aware that I was going to be late for my next class.

"Shoot, I gotta go, Sara. I'll see you tomorrow for lunch. We'll eat alone."

"Ok, bye, Rick."

I dashed down the hallway to my locker. To make matters worse, my books tumbled out of my locker. After fumbling with my bag, I finally got the books I needed and placed the others back into the locker. By the time I made it to class, I had the opportunity to meet the stone-faced Mr. Harold face on. This was going to be a tough session.

৪০

Yesterday, I felt full of energy. Life was taking a better turn. Sara met my friends. It didn't matter that she didn't say much. That would come in time.

I intended to make the most of each moment I spent with Sara. Time with her is limited, so I can't afford to take any of it for granted.

When Sara's bus pulled up, my heart leapt in my chest. I felt energy pulsing through my body pretty much the same as it did yesterday.

Then I saw Sara's face as she walked toward me.

Yesterday, there had been color in her cheeks. Even though she was nervous about sitting with my friends, her expressions were more alive than they'd ever been since I first met her. Sara seemed happy.

Today, Sara is the opposite of that. Her eyes are red and her cheeks look damp. Why is her skin pale? Is she afraid of something to come or rather to tell me about something that happened? Oh, God, please don't let it be that he hurt her again.

Sara wrapped her arms around my neck and wept. I held onto her, hoping I could bring some level of comfort for whatever bothered her.

"Tell me what's wrong," I pleaded.

"I don't want to tell you right now. I'll tell you at lunch."

I gently pushed Sara away. Her mouth quivered.

"I can't wait until lunch. I'll go crazy all morning. I really need to know now. Did he hurt you?" I asked, wiping away her tears.

"No. Nothing like that."

"What then?" I said, relieved.

"He's...he's taking us to the Poconos this weekend. We'll be there through Monday," Sara sputtered out.

Oh, no. He'll have them alone...all weekend. I gotta figure out a way to keep her here.

"Sara, you can't go."

"I have no choice. I'm scared, but I have to go."

"Maybe we could disappear for the weekend," I suggested, impulsively. I regretted saying it the moment the words left my mouth. Where would I take her and what would she do once he returned?

"And then what? I can't leave my family, Rick."

Sara walked away, but I grabbed her arm.

"I'm sorry. I wasn't thinking straight. I just want you to be safe."

"I know. I should go to my locker. Talk more at lunch?"

"Sure, Sara. See you then."

I let her go to her locker on her own. My chest hurt as I thought of her alone with that monster. I really can't remember much from my classes. The rest of the morning was one big blur.

When the bell rang for lunch break, I found my feet quickening their pace to the cafeteria, but it wasn't due to excitement. I didn't want to waste one moment away from her, especially since her immediate future was in peril.

What's strange is that once I sat across from Sara at our special table, I didn't know what to say to her. I held her hand while we ate in silence. Once in a while, Sara looked up at me and tried to smile, but the smile struggled under the strength of a frown. I can't imagine my facial expressions being any different. Finally, I broke the silence.

"It hurts to think of you so far away. I have absolutely no way of getting in touch with you to see if you're ok."

"My mom has a cell. If things get bad, I can call 911 – that's if we get reception out there. Don't worry, Rick."

"I don't think that's going to be possible, Sara. Shoot! You know, I really love you. I don't want you to get hurt. I wish there were something I could do to get you to stay."

"I think I'll be alright. If I don't mess up and my mom can cover for us, we should make it through ok. But…whatever happens, you'll be here for me when I return, right?"

I nodded and then I shrugged.

"I'll be here, but I don't want anything to happen to you. I'll be here no matter what."

"Thanks, Rick. That means a lot to me."

The bell rang.

Didn't we just get here? There's never enough time with her.

"I'll come to the music room after school. I can't stay long."

"I know, Sara. I'll meet you there so I can walk you to the bus."

෩

We held hands tightly as we walked to her bus. As we waited in line for Sara to get on, I turned to face her and tried to kiss her on the lips. Quickly, she put her hand up against my chest and turned her face to the side and looked down.

"I can't kiss you right now. I'm so sorry."

My body shook. It didn't make any sense.

"I thought you liked to kiss me."

"I do."

"Did you want someplace more private? We could…"

"No, that's not it," she interrupted.

A pit started to form in my stomach. Am I losing her?

"Sara, please. I don't understand why. If it's because you're afraid of getting me sick, I told you…"

"It has nothing to do with that," she said, quickly speaking over my last few words. "I just can't right now. I want to, but I can't. I don't know how to explain it. I don't want to hurt you. I'll do it if you really want me to, but…"

Oh, no. Am I being a control freak? There is no way I want to act like a monster too. I released her completely.

"No, I don't want it like that. It's ok," I murmured.

Her eyes furrowed, but her mouth turned down in a frown.

"Are you angry with me?" she asked sadly.

"No, why would you think that?"

"Because you stopped touching me. I said I couldn't kiss you, not that I couldn't hold you."

"Sorry, Sara. This is just so hard for me," I said, giving her a firm hug. "May I kiss you on the cheek then?"

"No, the hug is just fine."

Just then, the bus driver yelled for Sara to get onto the bus. She released me and backed away. My hands slid away from her back. I knew I would see her tomorrow, so why did this seem so much like a final good-bye?

"Can you do me a favor – let your hair out tomorrow?"

I felt like I was imposing.

"But only if you want to," I added.

"I can do that. And I'll kiss you tomorrow before I go. Bye."

I watched as Sara walked to her seat and plopped down next to her Goth buddy. I put my hand up to wave bye.

ADMITTING HYPOTHETICAL IS REALITY
৪০

I fought back tears as I drove home from school. From the way Sara looked on the bus, I imagine she did the same. I really miss her. I know I'll miss her even more this weekend. It's going to hurt.

Mom came home from the hospital and found me sulking as I sat at the kitchen counter. She pulled out the roast she had defrosting in the refrigerator and plopped it on the counter with a thud. I heard her sigh before she shuffled over to a stool near where I slouched and sat down facing me.

"Rick, tell me about this hypothetical girl of yours?"

"What do you want to know?" I murmured.

"Everything, but I'd like to start with her name and how you feel about her. I know you talk to Emma about a ton of stuff I never hear about. Let me in, Rick." Her tone had a sharp edge to it.

I frowned. "I talk to Aunt Emma because you're not around, Mom."

"Rick, that's not fair. I make myself available when I'm home. And you know you can call me at work in an emergency."

"Mom, I'm not trying to bring you down. I know you work hard to make sure we have what we need, but you're emotionally unavailable at the end of the day. Ever since Dad died, I felt I lost two parents."

Mom's eyes glistened, so I knew I hit a nerve.

"I'm sorry. I'm here now. Please talk to me," Mom pleaded, her tone softer.

I felt bad for making her cry. She works really hard. It's just that I miss her when she's away at work so much.

"Her name is Sara and I like her a lot," I answered, scratching my head hoping Mom didn't notice Sara means so much more.

"Hmm."

I'm busted.

"Have you two fooled around?"

"Fooled around? You make it sound like we were on a farm rolling around in the hay or something."

"Fine. Did you have sex with her?"

I shuffled in my seat. I knew where this headed. I mean…I never touched Sara that way, but talking to my mom about this stuff meant letting her into a part of my world I didn't want her nose sniffin' around. I sighed.

Then again, I suppose if I need Mom to help Sara, I'm gonna have to come clean about everything.

"C'mon, Rick. It's not a difficult question."

Shoot. I took too long to answer.

"No, Mom. I never had sex with Sara."

"Why did you hesitate? What's going on?"

"I…I want to…I guess, but I haven't, ok?"

"Ok." It sounded almost like a question, but Mom was thinking…too much. "Not that I'm saying it's ok, but you *do* know how to protect yourself if you do, right?"

"Yeah, yeah. I'm set," I tried to say as nonchalantly as I could, but my gut clenched tight.

Mom wasn't fooled. She glared at me and then looked at her ringing hands.

If it were up to Mom, I wouldn't have sex until after I turned eighteen. In fact, she would have me wait until my wedding night.

Sure, she is a Christian with fairly conservative beliefs, but I think because she's a nurse and the fact that a condom can break makes her overly cautious and a little scared. I know she's got a point, but I'm not going to tell her. This thing that I have with Sara feels too good to say I'll wait. But, on the other hand, I'm not sure Sara won't need to wait considering everything she's been through. I guess I haven't totally decided yet.

"Is that all you want to know? Whether or not I've had sex with her?"

"I just want to make sure you're being safe. I wish you had a man in your life to talk to."

"I don't need a man to talk to. I need you. I need you to be available and I need you to listen…without judgment. Mom, this is hard and I love her so much. I need your help to do this right – to save her."

Oh, snap. Did I just say 'I love' Sara? I stopped breathing briefly as I braced myself for Mom's next sentence.

"I can tell you adore her, Rick. It's written over everything you do and say with respect to Sara, but I'm not here to mess things up for you. I love you and just want you to be safe. I'd like to meet her, but I understand there might be some difficulty in doing so. Take your time and tell me what you know. Emma and I want to help, but we need to know everything."

I nodded in agreement, relieved. Mom knows me all too well. I told her as much as I thought necessary for them to help Sara. I talked about Sara's mom and siblings and about her step-father's abuse and threats. Lastly, I added the latest information about the upcoming trip. Mom listened patiently to everything I said to her. She tried to remain objective in her body language, but I could tell some of the details bugged her whenever she squeezed her hands tightly.

"I don't want Sara to go away this weekend. I'm afraid for her."

"I know, Rick, but we'll need to wait until after she returns to act, especially if we want to keep her siblings together."

"Ok, Mom."

Mom placed her hand on my shoulder.

"We won't stop until she's free of him. Don't give up hope. I love you."

"I love you too, Mom."

We embraced and I cried on her shoulder.

೮ঽ

When I got up the next morning, I felt hopeful that things would turn out alright now that both Mom and Aunt Emma were working together with real facts, instead of hypothetical people. Under any other circumstance, I think Mom would have been overjoyed at my having a girlfriend, but instead, she became nervous I would do something impulsive and get myself hurt.

Before I went to bed, Mom brought up STDs and wondered if I knew anything about Sara's step-father's medical health. When I explained that Sara and I were nervous about not knowing that information, Mom took a few deep breaths to calm herself before suggesting that both Sara and I be tested soon to see if we've been infected. The problem was testing Sara. It remained hard to get her away from her family. I suggested the possibility of inviting Sara back to Aunt Emma's shed, but Mom hesitated, saying it might be too dangerous to try such a stunt.

The traffic lights were kind to me today. It's as if they knew I couldn't handle any more difficultly. I parked the car and walked to the bus area of the lot. I stood waiting for Sara to emerge. When she stepped off the bus, her flowing dark, curly hair surrounding her cute face filled my vision. I could swear my heart skipped a beat...or two.

SURVIVING THE NIGHTMARE TRIP
ფ

When I stepped off the bus and looked at Rick's face, I swore he looked like he would faint out of joy. I spent the bus ride here unbraiding my hair as a gift for Rick before I went on the dreaded weekend trip with my step-father.

I grinned at Rick to let him know I was alright, and then we quickly embraced. I can't believe I have a boyfriend who's extremely understanding and tender-hearted...and patient. I love him. I feel elated when I see him, excited when he touches my hand, and I can almost feel light glowing inside when he kisses me. This has to be love that I feel or at least something as good.

Yesterday was hard. I left feeling like I ripped Rick's heart out by not kissing him. I know now I was just scared. After arriving home, I rushed into my bedroom and fell on my bed crying.

My mother rushed into the bedroom. "Hi, honey, what's the matter? Did something happen at school?"

I wanted so much to tell her the truth, but I knew she would tell Chuck when he beat her. So, instead, I said what she already knew.

"I hate it here. Why can't we leave? I can't even have any friends."

"Sara, you know it's not that easy. He'd track us down. We have nowhere to go. I'm sorry that all of you are suffering like this."

"Why did you marry him?"

"Shhh. Not so loud. He'll hear you. I don't know how much longer I can hold him off if you anger him again."

"Mom, I love you, but you created this. You've made my life a nightmare. You've sentenced me to death. Leave me alone."

I hated doing this to her. She was ravaged by Chuck and treated like dirt, but I hated more the fact I would be treated the same in about two months. I'm not so sure Rick would stay with me after that. How could he? How could anyone?

Mom left the room sobbing, passing Dontae in the hallway. He came into my room and closed the door.

"What's up with Mom? You don't look so good, either. What's up?" asked my brother.

Dontae and I used to talk a lot before we moved here when all of us kids shared a room. However, with the new sleeping arrangements, we haven't been able to say much. Chuck grows extremely suspicious if he finds us talking for a while.

"I have a secret," I began.

"You know I won't tell. Go on."

"I met someone at school I like very much. His name is Rick."

"Is he good to you?"

"Yes, he is. He's very sweet and kind, not pushy, very patient when he teaches me violin…and cute."

Dontae raised his eyebrows and smiled.

"He teaches you violin? Wow, that's cool. I'm happy for you, Sara. I have a friend too. Her name is Tess. She's cool and stuff. I'd like to hang out, but you know."

"Yes. Rick and I feel the same way."

"Is it serious with you two?"

"I think so. He's my boyfriend. Please don't say anything."

"Not to worry. You know my secret too, so there's no way I'm going to spill yours," Dontae said to reassure me.

"Good. You know what scares me most?"

"What?"

"That I'm not going to be able to keep him."

"Why do you say that? From the way you talk about him, it sounds like he'll give you anything you need."

"But I'm having a hard time figuring out what that is. I don't know what he sees in me. I'm so messed up inside."

"He sees what I do, Sara. He sees a girl who is capable of much love and has great musical talent. If he likes you at least as much as you do him, he won't be so quick to let you go without a fight."

"I hope so."

"I better go. I think Chuck's coming inside. It's going to be fine, Sara. We'll escape someday. You'll see."

I nodded before Dontae left my room and closed the door behind him.

My memory of last night melted into the pleasure I felt in the present. I must have shivered because Rick rubbed my back. When we released each other, he looked at me with concern written over his face.

"I'm alright. Now that I'm with you, I feel very good. Are you alright? I didn't leave you well yesterday."

"I feel great now that you're here. You're absolutely gorgeous, Sara," Rick said holding my hand, and I leaned my body close to his as we walked down the hallway.

My face grew warm. I still had trouble believing his words. It seemed more like the talk of a boy on cloud nine instead of with both feet on the ground, but it felt good to hear him say it just the same.

It's Thursday, the day before my family leaves on our trip. I intend on making today special. It may be the last day I'm this happy.

ଔ

In addition to eating, we spent lunch talking about music and relishing in our newfound relationship by holding hands. I was about to talk about the upcoming weekend when Rick's friend Taylor rushed up to our table.

"Hey there, hottie, like the hair," said Taylor.

I looked down at my plate while my face became hot.

"Cut it out, Taylor," warned Rick.

"No, I mean you look really pretty, Sara. You should wear your hair like this more often."

"Lay off. Stop flirting with my girlfriend, Tay."

"Is that what I'm doing? I don't mean to." Taylor paused before turning to me. "Sara, I didn't mean to make you uncomfortable, but you really look great. I guess it's a good time to walk away. See you later."

Taylor walked away like a puppy with his tail between his legs.

"Sara," Rick said, "are you ok?"

"Yeah, I'm ok."

Rick's mouth turned up at one corner.

"You know, Tay may have been blunt but he's right. Letting your hair down changes you somehow – you're more confident and you glow. I know you think I say you're beautiful because I'm your boyfriend, but I hope now that you've heard someone else say it you can believe that you really are…beautiful."

I didn't know what to say. Part of me wanted to believe Rick put Taylor up to it, but after seeing how Taylor's aggressive behavior upset Rick, I knew that couldn't be true. I tried to smile, but I think it came out weird. I looked down at my tray and continued to eat my lunch.

ಬಿ

As agreed, we met in the music room so we could have a few minutes of privacy before I left on the bus. Friday would be a strange day. Chuck planned on picking me up after school which meant Rick and I would only be able to meet for lunch. But, considering the apprehension we both felt about the upcoming weekend, I knew lunchtime would not be all too pleasant.

After the last bell, I walked quickly to our rendezvous and stepped just inside the doorway. I brushed my hair away from my face and tucked the strands behind my ears. I moved toward Rick until we were about two feet apart.

Rick reached out and took my hand gently into his, pulling me closer. Slipping his hand around my waist, he started kissing me. It made me feel wanted.

However, this kiss was different from others that came before. It made me feel things I never felt, made me feel more. As his soft lips moved against mine, I found myself wanting him in ways I shouldn't, I couldn't. My heart beat faster. Does this new desire make me a bad girl?

Rick's still kissing me, and I don't want him to stop. I thought of my step-father saying I would amount to nothing more than a slut. Is this what he meant?

Rick tightened his hold on me, and I likewise on him.

My desire for Rick seemed to shoot through my entire body. My heart pumped hard and my breathing, shallow. My knees felt weak.

My base instincts enticed me to run away, run away from this. I'm not allowed to feel good. I can't.

But...I want to stay with Rick. I want to be with him and have...*shhh...don't say it! Don't even think it.*

I shivered and Rick loosened his hold.

"I'm sorry," he said.

Why is he sorry? I want him although I know I shouldn't. What's happening to me? I'm scared.

"I shouldn't have pushed you this far," he continued.

"I'm ok," I said dreamily, trying to get my bearings.

Rick helped me get stable footing.

"I don't want you to confuse this with what happens at home."

"What do you mean? What are you talking about?" I asked, confused.

"You got scared."

Oh, no. I shivered, the way I do whenever Chuck touches me. Is that what happened to me? My body remembered fear?

"I'm sorry, Rick. I don't know why. I actually like kissing you," I apologized, meekly.

"I know you do. I can tell, but there's too much going on with you. I need to back off. I should protect you in whatever way I can, even if that means I slow things down."

Rick gave me a quick kiss before I buried my head into his chest.

"I want to be a good girl."

"You're already one."

I looked up at him.

"I love you, Rick."

I said it. I finally said it, and I meant it. My heart flutters when he's near and I long to see him when he's not around. This weekend is going to be hard.

"I love you too, Sara. Man, you're gorgeous. I love your hair like this."

I found myself staring at his mouth. I wanted him to kiss me.

He kissed me again, this time on my forehead. I felt ashamed for wanting more.

"Let's go. I'll walk you to the bus."

We got outside before he spoke again.

"I don't want you to go away this weekend. I'm afraid for you, out in the middle of nowhere with no phone of your own. I don't want him to touch you."

"I think we'll be ok. You help me be strong. I'm taking you with me," I said, patting my chest.

I got on the bus and he walked along side and stood outside my window. His eyes looked like they glistened. My Goth friend leaned back as I reached to touch the glass. Rick held his hand against the outside pane until the bus driver beeped the horn so Rick could safely back away.

We knew we would see each other at lunchtime tomorrow, but this was good-bye for us. Chuck planned on picking me up after school before our trip, and he would be prompt.

I closed my eyes and thought of Rick as I re-braided my hair on the ride home.

൭

I arrived at school dying to see Rick. I hoped he would be waiting for me like he did yesterday, but other thoughts fought that hope. Leaving was so hard yesterday. What if he couldn't face me because my not staying with him hurt so much? What if he suddenly thought my problems were a bit much for him to deal with? My gut clenched as I strained to see him. I didn't think I could go on if he changed his mind.

But he waited for me on the sidewalk, smiling. I smiled back although I knew he couldn't see me yet, my heart pumping a little faster. I stood up out of my seat before the bus came to a full stop.

Walking quickly toward him, I fell into his arms. I suddenly felt tired, having spent most of the night helping my siblings pack for the trip.

"I know it was just overnight, but I missed you," Rick whispered in my ear.

I didn't want Rick to stop holding me, but the first bell rang warning us that we would be late for our first class unless we got to our lockers right away. Rick smiled at me as he released me, but he held onto my hand so he could lead the way to my locker. A quick kiss on my cheek marked our morning 'farewell' until we saw each other again at lunch.

ℬ

Now that I could stare at Rick's face without rushing through the hallway, I noticed how worrisome he had become.

"You know, I'll be alright," I tried to reassure him.

"I know. I just don't like not being able to contact you to make sure, that's all," Rick admitted. "I wish there was some way I could come out there, but my mom has to work this weekend and my aunt has some cases to take care of."

I was shocked as the realization came over me that Rick talked to them about spending the weekend in the Poconos.

"You'd do that for me? Come out to a place you never planned on seeing?"

"Why not? I'd do anything to keep you safe."

I sighed and took one last mouthful of food.

"Good, you're finished," Rick said. "Let's find some place we can be alone before the bell rings."

"Ok," I said and quickly picked up my tray.

After leaving the cafeteria, Rick led me to an empty classroom.

"We should be ok in here for a few minutes. I just wanted to give you my goodbye kiss now, if that's ok. I figured I won't be able to after school."

"I'd like that, Rick. I didn't say anything this morning, but I missed you last night too. I think that will be the hardest part about this weekend, not being able to see you."

As I finished speaking, we heard the first of two bells, signaling the end of lunch. Without another word, Rick quickly pulled me toward him and kissed me. I lost myself in the kiss. I felt his soft lips against mine. I wasn't sure if I was keeping up with his energy, his passion. I felt his body tense as he kissed me more earnestly.

Then I felt tears against my cheek. They were mine. I suddenly remembered why Rick kissed me like this, like he might lose me somehow. I remembered and it made me sad. I didn't want to go and leave him, leave these kisses behind. These kisses proved that he cared about me and about what happens to me. What was going to happen to me in the Poconos? Would it be the beginning of my end? Would my hope of escaping harm be shattered the first night – the second?

The second bell rang. Rick reluctantly pulled away, desperately caressing my face. Tears ran down his cheeks too. They weren't mine, but they were for me.

"Sara, please be safe. Run away if you need to, please. Here's my cell number. Hide it where he can't find it."

"Ok, ok," I promised.

"We better go."

We wiped our faces as we left the empty classroom behind. Rick's expression showed he realized he didn't have enough time to walk me to my locker.

"I'll meet you at your locker after school. I know he'll be outside, but I'd like to walk you near the front exit. Is that ok?"

"I'd like that. I'll need that. Thanks."

"Great." Rick waved once as he backed away. Then he turned on his heels and ran toward his locker.

I ran to mine to collect my books, making it to class just in time for the class bell.

৪৩

I had a hard time concentrating on my class work all day. The classes after lunch were even harder than in the morning. I kept thinking about the tears on Rick's face. How could anyone love me that much when I didn't...I *couldn't*... love myself that way?

I stood in front of my locker pulling out all the books I needed over the long weekend. I looked over my shoulder and saw Rick standing by my side. I was so focused on my locker, I never heard him. Or was I focused on my fear?

"Hey, you need any help?"

"No, I got it. I'm hoping my books will keep Chuck off my back."

Rick gave a faint smile. I tried to smile back, but the muscles didn't feel right. I probably looked like a sick dog.

I closed the door of the locker and spun the dial.

"I need to hurry. He hates to wait."

"Let's go then. I'll carry those until the door," Rick said as he extended one arm to take the two books I carried in mine.

I handed them over, and then Rick intertwined the fingers of his free hand with mine. That made me feel closer, protected, if only for a few more minutes. We stopped about twenty feet away from the front entrance.

"You should give me my books now. I think I see his van out there."

"Here you go," Rick said, handing me the two books. "Come back, Sara. Please, come back to me," he begged, and then he kissed me on the cheek.

"Pray for me," I said. I kissed him on the cheek too.

"I will."

I started to move toward the door. Rick stopped me.

"I'll go first. That way I can watch you as you go to the van."

"Ok."

"I love you, Sara."

"I love you too, Rick," I said as he walked away, releasing my hand.

I took a deep breath, hugged the books to my belly, and walked out the door. I saw Rick sitting on the left, writing something in a notebook. I walked slowly past him, keeping my eyes on the ground straight in front of me. I wanted to say something to Rick, but that would be a huge mistake.

I opened the sliding door on the van, but Chuck told me to sit with him up front. I dropped my books and bag in the back and closed the sliding door before opening the front door to get into the front passenger seat.

"Hey, darlin', looking forward to the trip?" Chuck asked as he caressed my leg.

I shivered.

"Yes, it'll be fun," I said while looking at the side view mirror.

I could see Rick now that Chuck pulled away from the curb. Rick stood up. He wore his sunglasses, I suppose, so he could watch us without Chuck noticing. I continued staring at the side view mirror even when Rick disappeared from view.

Rick, I miss you so much. God, please keep me safe.

Everyone was waiting on the sidewalk in front of the house when we arrived. I was happy to get in back away from the monster that was my step-father. I can't believe I'm stuck with him all weekend.

Due to traffic, it took an extra hour to arrive at our cabin in the Poconos. We were away from the main road, secluded by the tall trees surrounding the property. Finding out I would be sharing a room with my brothers and sister made me happy...safety in numbers. All of us kids stayed together as much as we could.

It was actually a pleasant weekend. Mom and Chuck had some alone time. She actually laughed the few times I saw them outside together. Not hearing her scream at all during our little vacation seemed strange…though pleasant to my heart. Perhaps we'll really be ok after all.

That was before Chuck said we were not returning home on Monday. He felt an extra day or two would be good for us. *What is he planning?* Oh, God, I have no way of telling Rick about the change. He's going to flip…out.

RICK'S PANIC STRICKEN HEART
&

I walked away, leaving Sara in the hallway, after I kissed her one last time, after I told her I loved her. She asked me to pray for her, but what should I pray for? Should I pray that the van breaks down so they never go on this nightmare of a trip? Do I pray that some ailment takes him away from her?

No...I guess not. I want to, but I'll pray for her like she asks. I'll pray that God keeps her safe on this trip – that no harm comes to her or the ones she loves. I'll pray all weekend long for her.

I pretended to write in my notebook as Sara walked past me. I put my shades on right after I sat so that her stepfather couldn't see I looked straight at him. I noticed Sara tried to climb in back, but he waved at her to sit in the front.

The monster...if he touches her, I'll...

Sara got in the front seat and tried to sit as close to the passenger door as she could get. I noticed that she shifted uneasily. He must've touched her. I wanted so much to rush the van and take him out. But...I wouldn't last a minute. He's a big guy. How could Sara ever fight him off?

The van pulled away from the curb. I stood hoping he didn't notice my interest in their leaving. It didn't look like he did. I watched as the vehicle disappeared down the street. I ran my fingers through my hair and pulled at it in despair. My tears, streaming down my cheeks, took the same route as the ones that came a few minutes before as I sat pretending to write.

I hurried to my car and drove home, a little too quickly.

Dashing out of the car and into the house after unlocking the door, I rushed upstairs, heart beating wildly, and flopped onto my bed. I cried for what seemed an eternity. I cried until I fell asleep.

I woke up to Mom calling again for me to get up.

"Rick…wake up. You left the door unlocked and it doesn't look like you ate. What's wrong?"

"What time is it?" I asked drowsily.

"It's ten. You slept through dinner. Talk to me."

"He took Sara away today, Mom. I'm afraid for her."

"I know, Rick. Let's hope for the best, ok?" Mom said, grabbing me up into her arms.

I leaned helplessly onto her shoulder.

"Mom, I love her so much. I don't want him to hurt her."

"Shhh," Mom said, like she did so many times when she didn't know quite what to say, but I knew it meant she would stick with me through whatever.

We ate dinner very late that night.

∽

I rode past Sara's house every day that weekend, twice. I never thought of Columbus Day weekend being an eventful weekend except for sales, but this one was quite stressful. I hoped by some miracle that Sara's family would return early – no such luck.

Mom warned me not to go into their yard. She didn't want the neighbors thinking I was a prowler. I didn't want to listen. I just wanted to know that she could escape safely through her bedroom window.

I held it together until Monday, but when I drove by at six and didn't see the van, I lost it. I rushed home and begged my mother to call the police.

"We can't, Rick. We don't know anything is wrong and the police will want proof," Mom said, trying to comfort me by patting my shoulder.

"Mom, will rape or, worse, death be proof enough for them?" I screamed.

"Rick, please calm down."

"I'm not going to calm down. My girlfriend is out there with a monster! I'm going to Aunt Emma's. Maybe *she* can help," I said. I ran out the door.

However, when I got to Aunt Emma's house, she preached the same sermon to me. I didn't want to hear that I couldn't do anything for the girl I loved with all my heart. Didn't I tell her I would help her?

"Go home. They're probably still on the road coming home tonight. The Poconos are a long way off. Go to school tomorrow. Hopefully, you'll see her there," said Aunt Emma.

Reluctantly, I went home. Reluctantly, I went to bed and fell asleep.

The next morning, I hurried through my morning routine. I wanted to drive by Sara's house before going to school. However, when Mom got wind of what I was going to do, she warned me to resist exposing myself to Sara's father.

"There's no telling what he'll do if he sees you driving by. He may recognize you from Friday," warned Mom.

I knew she was right. I headed straight for school hoping to see her walk off the bus to greet me.

But there was no Sara, not in homeroom, not in our morning classes, not even at lunch. I asked all my friends if they had seen her, but everybody said 'no'.

Frantically, I called my mom at work. She often told me to only call her for an emergency. Well, in my mind, this counted as major.

"Mom," I said, my voice cracking, "she didn't come to school today. I'm really worried. Can you do something?"

"Oh, Rick, I'm so sorry she's not at school. We have to wait one more day."

"Why?"

"The hours-missing rule."

"As far as I'm concerned, she's been missing all weekend."

Who knows what he's doing to her? Did to her?

"But, according to the school, she's only missing today. Tomorrow, if she's not back, I will go with you to the police, ok?"

It wasn't ok, but I didn't have any proof other than Sara's story. The problem was she wasn't around to corroborate any of it.

After school, I drove by Sara's house – still no van.

I tossed and turned all night wondering what was happening to her. I woke up Wednesday morning with circles under my eyes. I looked like I'd partied all night. If only I had.

Once more, I raced to school hoping she would be on the bus. Then, I saw her standing, waiting her turn to get off.

She looked worried. All I wanted to do was hold her in my arms and tell her I still loved her no matter what.

I'm not sure what happened next, but instead of Sara greeting me at the door, her Goth friend took my arm.

"Rick," she said softly, "come with me. Don't look at Sara. Her father's here."

A pit rose in my stomach. My girl within reach, but I couldn't go near her, or her step-father would destroy her. I nodded, understanding.

"I know you want to look, but not yet," she said, leading me toward the school's entrance.

"Is she ok?" I asked, worry surfaced in my tone.

"She's fine. You'll see. She's not hurt," she assured me.

"Thanks for watching out for her, Ana."

"Hmm. You know my name," Ana said, surprised.

"Yes, I remember it from roll call. You don't say much, but I know you're a good soul. You're like an angel for Sara."

Ana smiled.

"I've studied you as well, Rick. Of all the guys Sara could have ended up with, you are the cream of the crop. You have a good heart."

I smiled then.

"Thanks. I didn't think you noticed."

"It's easy to notice things when everyone thinks you're weird and aloof. By the way, I plan on attending your recital in December."

I must have looked surprised because of what she said next.

"Yes, I like classical music too, but don't let that get out."

We stopped a few feet away from the door and allowed Sara to walk past us. Then, Ana took my arm again and walked me inside. I tried to loosen her hook on my arm, but she held firm.

"Not yet. He could be watching. Let's turn the corner first."

I knew she was right, but I increased the rate of my steps so I could reach Sara sooner. Ana went along with me. I hardly noticed the other students looking at us strangely. I'm sure to hear about this later.

When we turned the corner, Sara was waiting for me. I gave Ana a quick 'thank you' before zooming over to Sara.

I embraced Sara, almost knocking her over.

She grabbed my shirt to regain her footing, and then she slipped her arms around my neck.

"I'm so glad you're here. Are you alright?" I asked.

"I'm fine. I'm sorry you were worried. Chuck wanted to spend an extra day," said Sara.

Suddenly, Ana tapped me on the shoulder.

"He's coming toward the doorway. Rick, you need to come with me just in case he comes inside."

Ana tugged at my arm, but I resisted long enough to give Sara a quick kiss on the lips.

"See you at lunch," I said.

"Ok," agreed Sara, but she looked scared and worried all at once.

"C'mon, Rick," pressed Ana.

I let Ana lead me down the hall away from Sara. We crossed the hallway that led outside.

"Look at me, Rick," said Ana, while she looked past me toward the front door. "It doesn't look like he's coming inside. You should go to class just in case his suspicions bring him inside."

"Alright," I agreed and hurried to my locker.

I didn't see Sara at all until lunch, but thoughts of her were with me all morning. When I finally saw her sitting at our table, my heart felt warm and at peace. We held hands while we ate.

I asked Sara tons of questions, and she patiently answered every one.

Oh, how I love hearing her voice.

After we finished lunch, I led her out of the cafeteria, hoping to find a private spot. However, she pulled away at the last moment.

"What's wrong, Sara? Don't you want to be alone with me?"

"I do, but I guess I'm tired of being led everywhere. I'm back from a weekend trip I didn't want. I'd like to choose sometimes."

What Sara said hurt me. Was I being controlling? I guess I have been.

"Sara, I'm so sorry. I didn't mean to."

"I'm not upset, but do you mind if I choose sometimes?"

"Of course not. You can choose anytime you want. What do you want to do now?"

She walked toward me and kissed me on the cheek.

"I feel like my emotions are bursting out, so I want to take it slow for a bit, if that's ok."

I wanted to hold her in my arms. After this crazy weekend, I didn't want to slow down, not today.

"Ok, Sara. Anything you want," I said, but I was disappointed.

"I made you sad. I'll do what you want this time."

I realized what was happening. Her life was wrapped up in my own. She's happy when I'm happy. I need to set her free whether it hurts me or not.

"Sara, wait. I'll be ok. I don't want you to do things you don't want to just to please me. I'm glad that you told me how you felt. From now on, I'll try to ask instead of tell."

"Thanks, Rick."

Sara walked toward me and gave me the best hug ever.

SARA'S PREDICAMENT
&

We finally made it back home late Tuesday night. I still had Rick's number crumbled under the sole of my shoes, but I couldn't risk trying to call him from my house. I fell asleep quickly. It had been a long weekend with lots of hiking to avoid hanging around Chuck for too long.

My siblings also enjoyed the trip. We whispered to each other at night during the weekend that we couldn't remember the last time we enjoyed ourselves like this. The pleasantness of the trip surprised me. Chuck even tried to be nice…like a father almost. Was he trying to fool someone? What was he plotting? We had to make sure we kids did not let our guard down.

I got up early the next morning. I didn't want to be late. I knew Rick would be waiting for me at the bus stop.

Because of this, I nearly threw up when I realized that Chuck followed me in his car. I'm pretty sure the bus left him at home busy in the yard, but by the third stop, when I suddenly turned around to look out back, I saw him a couple blocks away.

"Oh my gosh. He's following me."

"Who? Who's following you?" asked my Goth friend.

"My step-father. Rick will be waiting for me. We didn't come back when we should. Chuck will beat me if he sees Rick greeting me at school. What am I going to do?"

I wasn't sure my friend got all that. I spoke faster than my own brain could comprehend. I even said too much. I said what was on my mind and heart. I was scared.

"Don't worry. I'll think of something," she said.

I couldn't think straight. My stomach heaved and hoed. I felt sick and my whole body heated up.

As the bus pulled into the parking lot, I saw Rick rush to my bus's usual spot.

What am I going to do?

I didn't want to ignore Rick, but I had no choice. My body shivered numerous times. I looked at my friend and I could see the worry on her face. She *never* looked worried before. *I'm doomed.*

Just then, my friend pushed past me.

"I'll go first. I'll try to explain. Walk straight into school and then you can talk to him," she said.

Relief showered over me. I didn't think she would do something like this for me. I didn't think she talked to anyone else. I thought she only talked to me out of pity. I didn't even know her name.

She rushed out of the bus and grabbed Rick's arm. The action startled him, but she kept him from looking at me. I couldn't hear what she told him at first, but by the time I caught up, I heard Rick say her name…Ana. Ana is my Goth friend.

I fell a little behind because I kept checking for Chuck's car. He parked at the far end of the lot and walked toward us. I kept my head down as I walked up the path to the front door. I recognized Rick's and Ana's shoes as I walked by, but I knew I couldn't ask them why they stopped. I had to keep going. She said she would bring him to me once I was inside. I walked around the corner toward my locker and turned around. This would be a good place to wait.

After a few seconds, Rick led Ana around the corner. He turned quickly to her and said something before he dashed toward me. I grabbed his shirt so I wouldn't topple over. Emotions welled up inside me. I felt like laughing, crying, screaming. I hugged Rick around his neck as tightly as I could without choking him.

Suddenly, Rick jerked away. Ana warned us that she saw Chuck standing in the doorway. Rick looked at me, concerned. I could tell he didn't want to leave me after not seeing me for so long, but knew he must. He kissed me on my mouth before leaving my side. Oh, that kiss, it left me warm all over.

Rick looked so tired.

How late was he up waiting for me last night or maybe even the previous night?

It would be lunch time before I saw my boyfriend. I would have to be patient.

Once at lunch, I told Rick everything, from the time I left school to the moment I saw him this morning. He was so relieved that I was not attacked this weekend, as was I.

After we finished eating, Rick wanted to go someplace so we could be alone. It's not that I didn't want to be alone. I wanted so much to kiss Rick, but deep in my gut, I felt some trepidation about being alone with him. I wanted to be the one to choose. I don't think he realized how much he took away that choice just by trying to be helpful. Or rather, how much I kept giving up that choice to him because I didn't want to hurt or lose him.

In that moment, I realized just how much I had changed since my childhood. I used to be independent and a free-spirit. Now, I cowered in the presence of my step-father. Rick just happened to be a more pleasant replacement. Will he be angry if I resist?

I took the risk and it paid off. Rick was very understanding. I could see he struggled with what I said, but he felt sad for threatening my well-being. He loved me that much.

I kissed him on the cheek, but I could tell he was disappointed. Perhaps I wanted too much of my own way. I didn't want to make him sad.

"I made you sad. I'll do what you want this time," I relented.

"Sara, wait. I'll be ok. I don't want you to do things you don't want to do just to please me. I'm glad that you told me how you felt. From now on, I'll try to ask instead of tell."

"Thanks, Rick."

I can't believe how much this boy loves me. He wants me to be happy too.

I walked toward him and gave him the best hug I've given anyone on the planet. He'd won all of my heart.

The bell rang, so we parted ways for the rest of the day. Because I couldn't stay after school this week – I didn't want to risk having Chuck find out especially if he tracked my movements – Rick and I agreed at lunchtime to meet in homeroom the next day. That way we could talk without fear of being found out.

That night, in my bedroom, I thought about how Rick had freed me, freed me from one of my prisons. As a human, I had the right to choose my path without fear of retaliation. I also learned that although others may hurt from my freedom, sometimes they are willing to accept that hurt because they've learned the benefit of that freedom.

Thursday was great. Chuck followed me to school again, but I was prepared this time. Rick walked straight to homeroom and waited for me there. He smiled at me when I walked through the door. My heart thumped a little faster.

I felt happy that I would see him throughout the morning in addition to lunch. We stole moments between classes to talk about music and the upcoming recital. I hadn't forgotten about the part I would play in Rick's recital, but I was worried that I wouldn't be able to practice as much as I needed.

In addition, Rick suggested I meet him at his aunt's shed on Saturday. He was very careful to let me choose which made me feel good inside. I agreed to meet him if Chuck did not become suspicious.

"If I don't show, it's because it's not safe," I said.

"I'll try to remember that. My mom and aunt may want to meet you too. Will that be ok?"

"Once I'm there, that should be fine."

03

I left Chuck working in the yard, getting it ready for bulbs, mums, and other fall plants. He gave me the usual stare, but made no other movements to suggest he would follow me. I kept checking at each turn just to be sure I remained alone.

By the time I reached Rick's aunt's house, half of my energy had been spent in worry. I was relieved to find Rick waiting for me in the shed, unlike last time when I arrived first.

I walked toward him and gave him a hug.

"Is it alright if we kiss?" he asked.

I smiled. His request sounded chivalrous.

"Yes, it's alright."

I leaned toward him, not waiting for him to make the first move. It had been a while since we kissed like this. I almost forgot how much it takes my breath away. I pushed him away before I lost my mind completely.

"Sorry. Too much?"

"No, just right."

"Are you ready to meet them?"

"They're in the house?"

"Yes."

I took a deep breath.

"I'm ready. Let's go."

Rick took my hand, and I followed him into the house. Two women sat on stools next to the kitchen counter. The kitchen, painted in white with flowery patterns along the ceiling, contained an island for chopping and a table with chairs for small meals. One of the women got up to greet us. I guessed that it was Rick's mother.

"Hi, I'm Rick's mom. You may call me Ms. Conner."

I was right.

"I'm pleased to meet you, Ms. Conner. And you must be Rick's Aunt Emma," I said, turning to the other woman now getting up from her stool.

"You're right, Sara. And you may call me Miss Emma, if you like."

"I'd like that very much."

I looked over at Rick who was smiling at me. He seemed pleased that the greetings went well. I surprised myself at how brave I came across, but they made me feel safe somehow.

Ms. Conner and Miss Emma asked me about my situation and I tried to summarize it as well as I could. I could see the changing emotions drawn on their faces as I waded through my story.

Ms. Conner also brought up getting tested for STDs. She gave me a quick run through of the ones that would be easy to detect during an outbreak, but she said a blood or urine test would be needed to check for others. I felt uneasy about a blood test. Chuck had a habit of checking arms and such for any drug use. However, I agreed to the urine test the next time I came over.

"I need to go now," I said. "Chuck will come looking for me if I don't get home soon. I'll try to come back next week. Thanks for doing this for me. I just want to make sure I'm not a danger for Rick."

"I appreciate that, Sara," Ms. Conner replied.

"I'll walk you out back," offered Rick.

When we got outside, Rick squeezed my hand.

"My mom doesn't let on, but she's really concerned about you. Let us know if you feel threatened, ok?"

"I will. Will you get tested next week too?"

"I think Mom wants me to do it sometime this week. She made an appointment for me already with my doctor."

I nodded.

"I better go. See you on Monday."

"Bye, Sara."

CB

After the weekend turned into a new school week, everything seemed to go back to normal, including the yelling and screaming at home. It was good to get out of the house for most of the day.

I met briefly with Rick everyday to practice some songs. I barely finished ten measures before having to rush down the hallway to make the bus on time. I always made it, except for Friday.

Every time I rushed out of the music room, Rick followed close behind just to make sure I made it on alright. Friday, I saw something I don't think I saw before. Rick had dread written all over his features. It seemed like he thought he brought death to me. I must admit, the thought crossed my mind that I had died the second I discovered my bus had left school for home.

My knees went weak. I didn't think I could run home today. Besides, I wouldn't make it, and Chuck would surely rape me tonight.

"C'mon, Sara, I'm taking you. Get in the car," Rick said frantically.

"It's no use. I'm done for."

"Not yet. Maybe we can catch your bus before it gets to your house."

Rick opened the door for me.

"The driver won't let me on."

"We don't know that until we try. We'll beg. Besides, if that doesn't work, I'm not taking you home."

"You know I can't abandon my family. Rick, you promised."

He scratched his head and then started the car.

"You're right. We'll figure something out. For now, let's try to get you on that bus. Show me where it goes."

I gave him the route and in two minutes we were one stop away from catching up. Rick detoured down another street so we would be ahead of the bus when it let off a few more students. I got out of the car and ran to the bus as it waited for the last students to cross the street. I banged on the door.

"Please let me in. I missed the bus, but I need to get on."

"You know I can't do that. You'll have to walk."

I fought the release of tears when Rick finally ran up behind me.

"You don't understand. She has to be on this bus. It's really important. Please," begged Rick.

Just then, Ana walked to the front of the bus.

"Let her on. I'll vouch for her. If you want to keep your count straight, I'll get off so she can get on. It's a matter of life and death," said Ana in a serious tone.

I hadn't realized how much she gleaned from my odd behavior. Ana knew more than I thought she did.

The bus driver snorted a curse under his breath before letting me on. I forgot to say bye to Rick, but I knew he wouldn't mind. He would be grateful I escaped harm.

I was saved from my doom by the space of five stops. I let out a huge breath as the bus pulled away.

THE ATTACK
&

November brought me one month closer to the day I dreaded most. It also brought the usual bad colds to my family. Elena and Joel, my sister and younger brother, had to stay home because of fevers. Chuck's rule was if one kid had to stay home, then all kids stayed home.

I still had Rick's number in my shoe, but I couldn't get away to call him. I could only hope that he wouldn't worry too much. However, I quickly threw out that thought when I remembered his reaction when we went on our weekend trip. I had to tell him somehow.

I have an idea.

If I could only get a note to Ana, I'm sure she would pass it on to Rick. The problem was Chuck. He'd been working nights lately which meant he always returned home in time for the bus to arrive.

Amazingly enough, Mom forgot to buy milk, so when Chuck got home Monday morning in the mood to eat cereal he was not happy.

"Woman, didn't I tell you to keep the frig stocked with milk?" he yelled.

"Yes, Chuck. I guess I forgot with the kids being sick and all. I'll go get some," stammered Mom.

"Never mind. I'll go buy it myself."

He stomped out the house and I knew I wouldn't have much time to write the note and get it to the bus. Also, given Chuck's mood, he was sure to speed to the nearest convenience store so he wouldn't be gone long.

I ran to my room after making sure Chuck drove away. I barely finished the note when I heard the bus rumbling down the street toward our house. Dropping the pen on the floor, I dashed toward the door and opened it. Mom gasped and screamed after me to come back into the house before Chuck returned.

"I will," I promised, "but I need to give a note to a classmate so she could make a copy of her notes for me," I lied. I hated lying to Mom, but I knew she would tell Chuck that I made friends when he beat on her. It's just better she didn't know.

I told the bus driver I just wanted to quickly give a note to someone. I rushed to the back of the bus, relieved to find Ana sitting in our spot. I offered her the note.

"Aren't you coming to school?" she asked, one eyebrow raised.

"I can't, not until the younger ones get better. Can you give this to Rick? I don't want him to risk coming over because he's worried about me."

"Sure, but…"

"I can't stay. He'll be back soon," I said, cutting her off. I turned around and rushed off the bus. I did not turn around until I reached the front door. I looked up and down the street for any sign of Chuck. His car had just cleared the corner.

I think I pulled it off.

I knew for sure Chuck didn't suspect anything when he quietly sat and had his breakfast. As expected, Mom didn't say anything. It looked like she accepted my reason for rushing onto the bus. I was safe…for now.

By Tuesday night, both fevers had broken, but Dontae and I had to wait until Thursday to go back to school because Elena and Joel were still too tired to last all day and Chuck wanted to keep track of all of us. Mom called all of the principals to say we were sick.

Because of our different schedule this week, Chuck decided he would drop off and pick up all the kids both Thursday and Friday. This meant no practice after school, and no time before school to mingle. I would be dropped off just in time for the first bell. Worse yet, I had to use my lunch hour on

Thursday to find out about all the work I missed earlier in the week. By lunch time on Friday, Rick was beside himself.

"I asked Ana about you every day when I didn't see you get off the bus. She gave me your note on Monday, but I was still worried about you. I even thought of driving by. She told me you finally came back yesterday, but I got held up by my music teacher when I planned to look for you. I tried to catch you after school and knew something was up when your step-father picked you up. Sara, you have no idea how much I missed you."

"I think I can guess. I missed you terribly too. I'm sorry I couldn't call you. I hate making you worry."

"Can we go somewhere so we can be alone? I don't want to push you, but I really need to hold you."

I wanted to say yes, but, again, I had to meet with another teacher.

"I can't, Rick. I have to pick up some papers for History."

"Then, can I see you tomorrow?"

I started picking up my tray.

"I'll try. Same time, but if I'm not there within thirty minutes, it just means I got stuck for some reason."

I left the cafeteria knowing that my answers didn't satisfy him. It was killing him knowing we couldn't spend time together outside of school unless I sneaked out, which was virtually impossible. The few times I met him in the shed was limited and, lately, had to be shared with his mom and aunt.

But it wasn't just hurting Rick. I wanted to be with him too. It was so bad that I even thought about sneaking out at night to see him.

On Saturday, when I headed for the door for my afternoon walk, Mom asked me to start on some laundry and house cleaning. I promised I would do it when I returned, but when she told me Chuck wanted it done right away, I knew I had to drop my plans of meeting with Rick. I felt like crying.

That night, around seven, I lay on my bed thinking about Rick when I heard something against the window. I thought it was just my imagination, but then I heard the same sound again. I got up and looked outside. I gasped when I saw Rick's face. I opened my window as far as it could go. Chuck was smart. He had barricaded our windows so we couldn't get out. It was just enough to let the stale air out.

"Rick, what are you doing here? You'll get me in trouble."

"Sara, I was worried and I wanted to make sure you're alright."

"Yes, now go."

"I need to talk to you."

"Not now, Rick, please. I hear someone. You have to leave," I pleaded.

"Aww, shoot," grumbled Rick.

"What? What happened?" I said, panicking.

"I think I crushed a plant."

Terror gripped my heart. Chuck noticed everything.

"Sara, unlock your door now!" yelled Chuck.

"I'm coming," I said loud enough for Chuck to hear. Then to Rick I softly said, "Hide."

By the time I got to the door, Chuck had gone out the front door. He came around back with a flashlight. When I searched outside my window, I didn't see Rick. I hoped he found a good place to hide. Chuck looked around the yard a bit.

Then my little piece of the universe was torn apart.

Chuck cursed. He found the crushed plant.

"Who were you talking to, Sara?"

"No one."

"Don't lie to me! Someone was out here!"

"Maybe an animal or something."

"Animals don't wear shoes, Sara. It's over. Your night is tonight."

"Please, no," I cried.

I ran to the front door yelling, but Chuck blocked my way and knocked me to the floor. Grabbing my hair, he locked the front door before dragging me, screaming, to his bedroom.

"Please don't hurt me," I begged, but he locked the door, with my mother pleading on the other side.

DISMAY
&

"Mom, you need to call the police now!" I quietly yelled into the phone.

I took a great risk trying to locate Sara's bedroom. I had let my wanting to see Sara get the best of me. I wanted to hold Sara in my arms and smell her hair. I wanted to kiss her soft lips and tell her how much she means to me. So, I snuck around Sara's house until I saw her through her bedroom window. I tapped on the window. I couldn't wait to hear her voice.

But I had screwed up, royally. I came to her house and ruined her step-father's garden. Now, he's going to do what we all dreaded most. He's going to rape her...tonight, because of me.

I hid when I heard the front door open. I slipped into the neighbor's back yard and prayed that he wouldn't see me. He didn't, but he found my footprint under Sara's window. She tried to lie, but it was no use.

I called my mom, but I know I wasn't making any sense. My voice cracked under the strain of trying not to cry.

"Mom, I can hear her screaming!"

Mom put me on hold while she called 911 on the land line.

"Mom, tell them to hurry. I think they're in his bedroom. Mom…"

I couldn't breathe. My voice sounded all wrong – high pitched.

"I'm going in."

"No you don't, Rick. Wait for the police!"

"Mom, I can't let her get raped."

"And I can't take the chance that he will kill you for breaking into his house. Wait. They're on their way."

I knew she wanted to ask me why I was stupid enough to go there.

I feel horrible for placing Sara's life in danger.

She's still screaming.

I can't see anything through the shades. Maybe, I don't want to see.

Sara …

THE FIGHT FOR SARA'S LIFE
℘

Chuck ripped all my clothes off and threw me on the bed. I struggled to get away while he tied my limbs to the bedposts. My feet met their mark sometimes, because I heard him grunt and curse whenever I hurt him. He paused, surprised, but my victory was short-lived. He slapped and punched me again and again. He grabbed me roughly, trying to get me in place for the final rope to be tightened.

I kept screaming, praying someone would come to save me from this. I hoped God would hear.

Rick, where are you? I thought.

I wanted him here to help me, but I didn't want him to see me like this – naked.

Having tied me to the bed posts, Chuck ripped his shirt off. He started to work on his pants when I heard sirens outside the house. I wasn't sure Chuck heard them. Or maybe he did, and he just wanted to finish what he started. He jumped on top of me, still trying to get the zipper down.

I kept screaming, but I couldn't push him off. He had me trapped. I hoped that whoever was out there would come in here now.

As if in answer to my prayer, as soon as Chuck finally pulled down his pants, someone knocked in the bedroom door and pulled him off. I couldn't tell, but I don't think he penetrated me. At least, I hoped not. Everything happened too fast to tell, and I hurt everywhere, anyway, from all the blows.

I heard a scuffle in the living room, but I was crying and couldn't hear much beyond the sound of my voice. I struggled against the ropes. I wanted to cover myself. I didn't want anyone to see me like this, see me totally exposed for all to gawk.

Suddenly, someone entered the room, but I couldn't see anymore. My eyes were swollen and wet with tears. However, I heard a voice, a woman's voice, and it was kind.

"It's ok. You're alright now. I'm a cop and I'm going to cover you up and then remove the ropes."

The relief my body felt at those words and the feel of a sheet covering my nakedness resulted in a series of sobs, sobs that seemed to never end.

THE RESCUE
ॐ

I could hear Mom talking to Aunt Emma after she hung up the 911 call. The sirens drew closer each second. I wondered if they would get here in time.

My mother warned me to stay hidden until she arrived so I wouldn't be mistaken for a burglar or worse, an accomplice.

When I saw the flashing lights nearing the house, I ran through the neighbor's yard to access the street perpendicular to the one Sara's house was on. I ran around the corner just as Mom and Aunt Emma pulled up in their cars.

The cops were already inside. I didn't hear any more screaming, but I wondered if they had arrived in time. My heart heaved at the thought of the worst outcome.

Two cops escorted a resistant Chuck, in handcuffs, to one of the cop cars. Sara's mom was being questioned by another police on the porch. I tried to look inside, but a fourth cop blocked my way.

Mom walked up and explained that she, a nurse, made the call and would help as needed. Aunt Emma asked about the children who had been huddled in the far corner of the living room, but the cop explained that everyone would be sent to the hospital for examination.

I tapped my mom on the shoulder, and she knew exactly what I wanted to know.

"What about the girl?" Mom asked one of the cops.

"Not sure. An SVU cop is talking to her right now," he said.

"A what?" she puzzled.

"Special Victims Unit."

"Was she…"

"Not sure, ma'am. She's a bit delirious. An examination will be able to give you that answer," he explained and then walked away.

Mom looked at me with love, concern, disappointment, and fear all at once. I knew I needed to explain.

"Mom, I missed her so much. I wanted to see her. I could never forgive myself if he raped her."

"Rick, I know your reaction is normal, but please realize you are not to blame for this man's actions. He would have used any reason to move up her date. Focus instead on this – she is free of him now. She won't have to be afraid anymore."

I hugged my mom tightly. I wanted to believe things would be ok. I wanted to believe that, if she had been raped, she could bounce back and still want me in her life. What if she never wanted to see me ever again?

I saw the paramedics take a stretcher into the house. When they came out, Sara was wrapped under the sheets. I ran over to her side.

"Back away, young man," warned one of the paramedics.

"She's my friend. I just want to see her," I pleaded.

My mom showed her nurse's badge, so they let me by.

"Just a minute. She's badly hurt."

I shuddered.

"Sara, I'm here. I'm sorry."

"Not your fault. Love you," said Sara, weakly before she closed her eyes.

Her face was swollen from the beating he gave her. What other bruises did she endure?

"I love you too," I said before they loaded her into the ambulance and drove away.

After finding out which hospital they were taking the family to, I ran home to get my car. Mom said she would go straight to the hospital, and Aunt Emma said she would meet us there after she readied her house for the family.

"There's no way they could sleep in that house, not after what happened there tonight," said Aunt Emma before she got into her car and drove away.

Sara was still being examined when I arrived at the hospital. I still didn't know if she was raped. All I wanted to do was see her, talk to her.

When Sara's mom saw us, she walked over to give us the news.

"Thank you so much for calling the police. I can never repay you," said Mrs. Walsh.

I knew Sara's mom had been through a lot, but I needed to know now.

"How's Sara? Is she ok?" I asked.

Sara's mom looked at me, puzzled.

My mom came to the rescue.

"This is my son, Rick. He's Sara's boyfriend."

"Boyfriend? I didn't know…" Sara's mom trailed off.

"She kept it a secret so she wouldn't get into trouble," explained Mom.

Now, I was getting impatient.

We could explain all this later, after I know how Sara is doing.

Sara's mom looked at me. I think she could tell I struggled greatly.

"Sara is doing well. She was beat up pretty bad, but she'll heal in time."

"Did he…? Was she…?" I fumbled. I couldn't say the word. I couldn't say the stinkin' word.

"No, the examination showed the cops arrived in time. She was so distressed she couldn't remember. She's been crying a lot. But the exam showed that she wasn't raped."

Relief washed over me.

"Can I see her? Is it ok yet?" I asked.

"I think it should be ok in a few minutes. She'd been calling for you, but I didn't know a Rick, so I thought she was hallucinating. I'll talk to the doctor about letting you come back with me."

"Thanks," I said, trying to smile.

After pacing the emergency room for fifteen minutes, I was finally able to see Sara. She looked so tired and weak. Black and blue marks covered her face. Everything was swollen, including her lips.

"Hey there, Sara, how are you feeling?"

"Everything hurts. I'm glad you're here. It's not your fault, ok?"

"I messed up. I'm so sorry. I just had to see you."

"I know. I wanted to see you too. It's been a crazy week." She swallowed. "The doctor said he didn't rape me, so that's good, right?"

"Yeah."

"All I can remember is him being on top of me, but then everything happened too fast."

"It's ok. You're going to be alright. That's all that matters. He can't hurt you anymore."

"Right," Sara agreed. Her voice was so weak. "I don't have any broken bones, but I don't think I can walk."

"If they release you tonight, I can carry you."

"Sweet, but I think they're keeping me overnight for observation."

"Oh."

"Mom said your aunt can have us stay over her house for a while."

"Yeah, she's been working on that ever since I told her about you."

"Tell her thanks, ok?"

"Sure."

"I'm really tired."

"I better go so you can sleep. I'll see you tomorrow."

"Kiss me first."

I didn't want to hurt her. Sara looked so fragile now. Slowly, gently, I leaned over and kissed Sara's lips. I could feel the heat from all the blood that pooled there.

"I love you, Sara, more than you'll ever know."

"I think you clued me in over the past few weeks. Bye," she said, her eyes starting to close.

"Bye, beautiful."

"Hmm," moaned Sara, and I watched her drift off to sleep.

After I left her side, I helped Aunt Emma drive Sara's family to her house. Aunt Emma explained to Mrs. Walsh that she and the kids were welcomed to stay there as long they needed.

Pulling me aside, Aunt Emma gave me a heart-to-heart talk. "Rick, there's really no good time to bring this up, so I'm going to do so now. Sara has been through a huge ordeal. It's going to take her some time to learn what 'normal' should be in her life. I know this will be hard now that she's free to go out with you, but you must try not to have sex with her."

"Um, Aunt Emma, this is weird."

"I know and I wouldn't even mention it except she needs time and she needs to know that she doesn't have to give it up just to gain real acceptance from a guy. She needs to know you love her without that kind of physical touch. Do you get me?"

"Yeah. Actually, I do."

I walked away mulling over what Aunt Emma said. I didn't like what she said I couldn't do. I felt like whatever I did would be judged harsher because of what Chuck did to

Sara. I hated having all this responsibility placed on me. I just wanted Sara and me to have fun without worrying about her, as my aunt would say, "mental health".

But I knew I would try to listen. Aunt Emma really knows her stuff. I had trouble sleeping, thinking of Sara alone in the hospital. Mom gave me some Chamomile tea to calm me down enough so I could drift off.

FIGHT TO SURVIVE
ಐ

The next couple of weeks were hard for me. We stayed at Rick's aunt's house following the attack and Chuck's arrest. Aunt Emma said it should help me not being in our own house for a while. I still had nightmares though.

I loved Rick's aunt. She talked to me every day to find out how I felt and about the nightmares I had at least twice each night. She suggested I see someone, but I didn't want to do that. I felt scared.

My mom, brothers, and sister fared better than I did, probably because they all decided to see a psychologist to help them deal with everything that has been happening to us over the past few years.

I stayed away from school during that time, so Rick brought home all my assignments and handed in my homework for me. Fortunately, I didn't miss any tests. Miss Emma thought I should return to school Thanksgiving week to get back on my regular schedule. I dreaded the idea of everyone looking at me funny. Of course, that was the week we moved back into our home. Miss Emma needed more time to rearrange her house for our longer stay, and Mom figured we should live in Chuck's house up to the date the mortgage was paid, which was December thirty-first.

Needless to say, my nightmares got worst.

When I finally went to school, the welcome I received was much better than I expected. The newspapers talked about an attack, but no one knew the details. Everyone had only kind words to say.

The best part of all was being able to spend tons of time with Rick. We finally had a real date. He took me to see a movie. Knowing I needed a good laugh, Rick chose a comedy. By the time we left the theatre, my abdomen hurt, but I felt happy. I had no fear about retaliation when I got home, and I knew I could see Rick the following day if I wanted to.

We stood in front of Miss Emma's house in anticipation of our good-night kiss. However, I wanted privacy, away from curious eyes, and I wasn't quite ready for him to leave.

"Rick," I said, "I'm not ready to go in yet. Can we go somewhere? I want to be alone with you."

"Sure."

Rick took my hand, and we made our way to the shed behind his aunt's house. As we walked, I held onto the hem of Rick's shirt. I didn't want to lose hold of him. I also didn't know what to expect, which was a little unnerving, but I knew Rick wouldn't hurt me.

After we entered the shed, Rick turned to face me. He pushed my hair back away from my face. Then, he leaned slowly toward me, so he could kiss me. It occurred to me right then how much I had missed this. Rick kissed me with such care and passion I had not felt before. I knew without a doubt I loved him too.

Gradually, he pulled away.

"I'll put the blanket down."

Oh, my. Is this it? Does he want me now? I thought.

I watched him snap the blanket and lay it on the ground. I didn't move. I'd temporarily forgotten how. After he smoothed the blanket out, he returned to my spot to fetch me and led me over to it.

We knelt facing each other, our knees touching. After we sat on the blanket, Rick touched my face.

"You are beautiful, Sara."

I looked down at my knees, but he immediately, yet gently, held my chin so he could raise my head.

"I know you don't believe it yet, but you are *very* beautiful, inside and out."

Rick kissed me gently. I felt my body slump backward until I lay on the blanket looking up at him. Closing my eyes, I felt his hand slip under my waist.

Suddenly, Rick's hand hesitated and he stopped kissing me. I opened my eyes to find Rick sitting uneasily on his heels and looking down at me. I felt confused and tried to understand his changing expressions.

Did Rick want something else from me, something more?

I sat up and started shoving my blouse off one shoulder, but Rick touched my hand.

"No. Don't," he said.

"But I'm ok. Your mom said my blood tests all came out clean."

"I know."

"Then why not? I love you. Isn't this what I'm supposed to do?"

Rick shook his head. "Some people wait until they're married. Others don't. Our first time shouldn't be on this dirt floor in my aunt's shed." He kissed me again, thoughtfully. "Do you understand how much you mean to me?"

"A lot?" I answered.

"Yeah. A lot. You mean too much to me for us to do it like this. Besides, you don't have to prove your love for me. I already know you love me."

"You don't want me?"

"That's not it, Sara. I want you so very much." He touched my face. "But it's not the right time."

"Rick, I don't understand," I said.

"I see lovemaking as a time when two people can express their love for each other…when the time is right. I love you very much…but…it's not the right time."

"How will we know when the time is right? Why isn't it right, now?"

"Gosh, Sara, you can't imagine how much I want you. But with everything that's happened, I think it would be best if we take it slow. It's not the right way or the right time. Our first time should be special. I would want you to know we made love because we, well, are in love.

"Besides, I think you need more time to process what happened."

I must have done something wrong.

"Why? Did I tense? Did I shiver? Rick, I didn't fold my arms."

"No, none of those. Can you honestly say you're ready for this? Do you know that just because we're on a date doesn't mean we have to do this? It's ok. I can wait 'til the time is right."

I don't want to lose you, especially now.

"Will you still love me like you do now?"

"Of course. You have my heart."

What Rick said made me feel better. I threw my arms around his neck and he placed his arms around me, giving me a gentle squeeze.

"Ok. I think I get it."

He loves me. Nothing more is expected. It feels strange.

"Good. We better go before my aunt wonders about us."

"Can we go on another date soon?"

"Sure. Maybe we can go out next Saturday. Would that be ok?"

"Yes."

I felt sad to see him leave, but in my heart I knew I meant the world to him. Rick meant the world to me too.

We also practiced for his recital. Rick brought some instruments to my house, so I could practice often. If I got stuck, he did not hesitate to run over to my house to help me out. I wondered what Mom thought about him doting on me as much as he did.

Rick was always there for me. As I lay in my bed at night, I often wondered why he loved me so much. I had become damaged in my mind and in my heart. I didn't want to be me. Why did he want to be with me?

On Thanksgiving eve, Rick stopped by to bring a roaster pan. Mom volunteered to cook the turkey, but not having one, Ms. Conner said she would loan it to us. I didn't care what brought him over, I was always happy to see my Rick.

We sat on the porch as I leaned against his chest.

"Why do you even want to be with me? When I look in the mirror, all I see is an ugly girl trying to be with the most beautiful boy I've ever known."

"It's not true, and until you see that for yourself, all you'll see is what you believe."

"Why do you love me?"

"I love you because you fill my heart," Rick admitted, and then kissed my head.

"What do I have left to offer? Chuck stole my soul."

"He didn't steal it. He marred it. Now you need to heal. You'll still have scars, but you'll be stronger for it, wiser. You'll be able to understand how to help others who experienced what you did.

"Also, you have a passion for music that enriches the soul - mine, even your own. I want so much for you to see how much beauty you bring to life, beauty from inside you."

"I can't see it," I said, sitting facing Rick now.

"I know. Aunt Emma says she can find someone to help, but you have to go after it. I can't do this for you."

I sighed and hugged myself.

"There you go again," huffed Rick.

"What?"

"Hugging yourself. Anytime you're forced to face something new, something challenging, you embrace yourself."

"Why is that so bad? I need to feel held, supported."

"No, Sara, it's comfortable. You hold onto what you know because it's comfortable even though it's killing you from the inside out. You're gonna have to let go or you're gonna die in your comfort," Rick admonished me, raising his voice a bit.

I've never heard him talk to me like this. My skin suddenly felt clammy. I shivered.

"That hurts, Rick. Why are you talking to me like this?"

"Because you need to wake up, Sara. You have the rest of your life to live. Chuck was a monster to you, but now he's out of your life. Now, you need to rid the monster that lingers in your head. You carry him with you, giving him power. Throw him out, Sara," Rick pleaded.

"Rick, I don't know if I can do what you're asking," I whimpered, tears running down my cheeks.

"Listen, Sara, I have to go now, but I'm always available," Rick said, pointing to his cell phone.

He leaned over and kissed me on the forehead.

"Please don't go," I begged. "Don't leave me like this."

"You need time to think. Call me later if you need to."

Rick turned and walked away. I buried my head between my knees and wept.

HEARTACHE SHARED
୫

I can't believe I spoke to Sara like that. I can't believe I told her the things I did. It didn't sound like me. I don't know who that was.

I walked to my Aunt's house trying to figure out why the ache in my chest wouldn't go away. It wasn't until I arrived at her front door that I realized I felt heartbroken. I rang the doorbell. Aunt Emma opened the door.

"I just came from seeing Sara. I broke my own heart, Aunt Emma. I broke my heart when I told her she had to do more than just survive with the memories of her abuse."

I touched my wet cheeks and quickly shook the tears off my fingers.

Without a word, Aunt Emma reached out to me and hugged me.

"Then I walked away. She was crying. I want to help her, but I don't know that I can do this."

"Rick, you are helping her. She needs to do this for herself, not for you or anyone else. Sara has to find the strength to fight the demons in her mind."

I pulled away from the embrace and looked at my aunt's eyes.

"Aunt Emma, the way she looked at me when I was leaving, like I betrayed her, like I betrayed my love for her. How can I be helping her? I feel like I just destroyed her."

Aunt Emma grabbed my hand that was clutching at my chest and led me to the sofa to sit.

"Rick, there will be no easy stage to her healing. Most of it will be painful. The main thing is to always be available, but not always present. She will want you to be her guardian. You can't be that for her. If something ever happened to you or your relationship with her, she would fall apart. Sara has to stand on her own."

"I think I understand, but she's experiencing so much pain right now. I didn't want to leave her alone."

"I know, but you did the right thing and you need to stay firm about that when you see her. She needs to stand on her own two feet. She needs to ask someone else for help. I don't doubt that you'll always want to be there for her. However, if you're the only one she has to lean on, her pain will destroy you both."

The thought of that was too much for me. I leaned against my aunt's shoulder.

"Go home, Rick. Talk to your mother."

"Should I call Sara? Tell her to come to you?"

"No, let her do it on her own. She knows I'm here."

I frowned and looked at my clenched fists. I sighed.

"Alright. I'm going home."

A CRY FOR HELP IN DESPERATION
ೞ

After Rick left me on the porch, I cried until the world looked blurry around me. Wiping my eyes in the hem of my skirt, I stood up, deciding that I wanted more than these many tears in my life. I wanted Rick to stay with me. I would fall apart if he felt he couldn't.

"Mom, I'm going to Miss Emma's house. I need to talk to her."

Without waiting for a response, I ran down the street until I reached that familiar walkway. I stopped abruptly and strolled up the steps. I knocked softly on the door. So softly, I was surprised when she immediately opened the door.

"Hi, Sara. I was hoping it was you. Rick just stopped by on his way home."

Tears started flowing down my cheeks and dropped on my blouse.

"I think I pushed him away. I lost him, Miss Emma. Please help me get him back."

Miss Emma pressed her lips in a straight line and directed me to her living room sofa. I don't think I noticed the patterns of roses on it before.

"Sara, Rick cares about you very much. He just wants you to be well."

"Why did he walk away from me? He raised his voice. He's never done that and the things he said, they hurt so much. I need him now more than ever," I said grabbing her forearm.

Miss Emma sat thoughtfully for a moment before giving her response.

"Sara, tell me something. Do you believe Rick loves you?"

"Yes, but I don't deserve it, so I'm scared when my mess pushes him away."

"Sara, what do you think you could do to deserve Rick's love?"

"Maybe if I wasn't soiled by my step-father. Maybe if I didn't cry so much. Maybe if I didn't hug myself all the time."

When I said the last phrase, my fountain of tears seemed to replenish itself and a new flow of salty water sprung from my eyes. Miss Emma continued.

"So you think if you did everything right, you would deserve Rick's love."

"Yes," I blubbered.

"Sara, there is nothing a baby can do to deserve a parent's love. We love domesticated pets although we spend many hours cleaning up after them every day. Also, God couldn't love us any more if humanity displayed perfection in every area.

"Love is a gift. It's not something you earn. It's not something you work for. Rick loves you because you are Sara. He found out you existed and his love flowed up and out of himself to you. There is nothing you need to do now or in the future to make him love you. Does this make sense?"

I nodded.

"Do you believe it?"

"I want to."

Miss Emma paused to really look at me.

"Ok. That's a desire we can start with. Do you want to heal?"

"Yes. I do. I want to get better for Rick."

"Sara, listen closely to me. You can't do this for Rick, or for your family, or anyone else. You need to do this for you and you alone. I am a strong advocate of selflessness, but of all the times I dare to condone selfishness, it's now. You need to do this because you're that important. If you get help for any other reason, you're almost guaranteed to lose the things you want most. Rick loves you, but he can't carry you indefinitely."

Oh gosh, that's what I've been doing. I've been expecting Rick to carry me, to be my world, to be my reason for living. That's too much for any human to bear.

"I understand. What do I need to do?"

"Are you willing to get help from me or others I send you to?"

I nodded again.

"Ok, then. Go home and I'll call you tomorrow before we meet for Thanksgiving dinner."

Willingly, I got up and returned to the house I dreaded the most. I wish we didn't have to go back. I wish we didn't have to wait until the mortgage runs out. Miss Emma said she would let us live with her, but that it would be best to give her some time to adjust to a bigger family. I understand, but I have nightmares every night after I walk past the monster's bedroom. My mom sleeps with me now, but I still see him.

I tried not to look as I walked past the room where I almost got...where Chuck attacked me. I shuddered. I ran quickly to my room and shut the door. I need Rick and I need him with me now.

He said he would always be available to me, so I called his cell.

"Hello, Sara. Are you okay?" Rick said when he answered the phone.

"Rick, I need to see you. Can you come over…please?"

"You know I can't, Sara. I can see you at Aunt Emma's tomorrow. Otherwise, we gotta wait 'til Saturday."

"I can't wait 'til then. I need you now."

"No, Sara."

I don't know what happened to me. All I know is that I threw the phone across the room. Fortunately, my closet was open, so instead of crashing against the door, the phone hit my clothes and bounced off the side of my hamper before it hit the floor.

"What did I just do?"

I ran to the closet and picked up the phone.

"Rick, are you there?"

"Yeah."

"I'm so sorry."

"Your anger got the best of you, didn't it?"

"I'm really sorry, Rick. I didn't mean to…"

"Sara, you need to get help from the people who can."

"I need to know you still love me. When you left tonight, I got scared. It felt like you gave up on us."

"I haven't given up on us, Sara. I still love you deeply, but you need to see yourself as you really are and not the way Chuck saw you. I'm tired of fighting him. I want you…and only you. Do you get me?"

"Um hmm," I mumbled, trying not to break down in tears again.

"I'll see you at Aunt Emma's tomorrow, ok?"

"Ok. Bye, Rick."

"Bye, love."

The next day, on Thanksgiving, Miss Emma called as she promised to tell me that she had set up an appointment for me tomorrow afternoon.

"Someone can go with you if that'll make you feel more comfortable," assured Miss Emma.

"Can Rick come with me?" I hoped.

"Um, that's probably not such a good idea."

"Ok, can *you* come with me?"

"I think that would be possible. I'll pick you up at two o'clock tomorrow."

"I'll be ready."

On Friday, we arrived at the counselor's office at two thirty to fill out paperwork and wait for my three o'clock appointment. I felt so nervous, but Miss Emma patted my hand to calm me.

As we entered the counselor's office, she motioned for us to sit on the sofa opposite her chair.

"How do you feel about our meeting, Sara?" said the counselor.

"Oh…I don't know."

"Did you want to come here today?"

"No." I looked at Miss Emma to see if she was upset, but she showed no signs of any emotion.

"Why?"

"I didn't know if I could trust you."

"Do you think you can now?"

"I'm not sure yet."

"Ok, well, we can work on that. It's important for our sessions that there's some level of trust. Who do you trust the most right now?"

"Rick. He's my boyfriend."

The counselor slowly scribbled something on her pad.

"How do you feel about your biological father?"

My heart jumped. I didn't expect to talk about my dad.

"I really miss him. I loved him a lot."

"What about your step-father?"

I felt my face heat up and I started to perspire and shiver.

"I hate him, and although he's locked away, I'm still afraid of him. Any thought of him scares me."

"And Rick?"

I thought about Rick and a calming spell came over me. I felt a smile on my face.

"I love him."

"Why do you trust him?"

"He cares about me. He listens to me and wants me to be well," I said, pointing to my heart and forehead.

"Sara, I'm going to ask you something extremely personal, because I need to understand the relational dynamics. Let me know if you need to pass, ok?"

"Alright," I agreed, hesitantly. I looked to Miss Emma for assurance that she would protect me if I need her.

"Have you had sex with Rick?"

Suddenly, I felt uncomfortable with Rick's aunt sitting there. She shifted in her seat.

"I can leave if you need me to," said Miss Emma.

I shook my head.

"Please stay. I'll answer." I turned to face the counselor. "No," I said.

"Why were you nervous?" asked the counselor.

"I wasn't sure if Rick would want me to say," I confessed.

"Do you need approval from Rick?"

"Yes," I admitted.

"Is there a reason why you two haven't had sex?"

"He said we should wait for me to get better."

"Hmm, interesting for a boy his age. Why do you think he wants to wait until you get better?"

"I guess he talked to his aunt," I said pointing to Miss Emma, "but I'm not sure."

"What do *you* want?" probed the counselor.

"I'm not sure. I want to, I guess. But then, I don't know," I said, feeling flustered.

Miss Emma turned to me.

"Sara, I won't divulge anything you say at this meeting to anyone, including Rick."

I nodded and I think I said a meek "okay", but I'm not so sure. My nerves had the best of me.

The counselor put her pen down and clasped her hands.

"Before you leave, I just want to mention something. It's great that Rick is so in tune with your best interest, but one of your goals should be to grow emotionally so you can do that for yourself."

I knew she was right. It's what Rick had been trying to tell me, but I wasn't sure if I were ready to take that leap.

ৎ৩

On Thanksgiving, the day before the counseling session, it was the best turkey dinner I remembered ever having. Rick carved the turkey and I got to help Miss Emma bake pumpkin pie. I couldn't remember feeling so happy. Before leaving, Rick promised to call me Friday night to discuss plans for Saturday.

On Saturday, Rick stopped by the house. He called the night before to check on my counseling session. I gave him a quick summary of the things I discussed with the counselor.

"I think you need to do something special tomorrow. How would you like going to the shore with me tomorrow?" asked Rick.

"The beach? To swim?"

"No silly. I want to try something I think will help."

"Are we going alone?"

"Yes. Is that a problem?"

"No, alone is alright."

"I'll pick you up at nine."

"I'll be ready."

So here we were on our way to Cape May. It took over an hour to get there, but the scenery during the ride was beautiful although most of the trees had shed their leaves. After we arrived in the quaint town, Rick parked near the beach. It was quiet with most residents still relaxing at home when we walked onto the sand. I looked out at the dull blue ocean and took a deep breath of fresh air. The sea breeze tickled my lungs and enhanced my senses. The cool, crisp wind made me shiver. I was glad I wore my hoodie.

Rick took my hand and led me closer to the water. We both looked out over the crashing waves.

"Sara, you are phenomenal."

I looked at him in disbelief and then looked back at the ocean.

"Did you hear me?" Rick said, stepping between me and the ocean. "I said 'you're phenomenal'. I so wish you could see what I see in you.

"I brought you out here so you could hear the music that was created in nature for you. You seem to have a special connection to music. I told Mom about it. She believes it's your gift from God, and I think I agree with her.

"Now sit, close your eyes, and listen to the music."

I doubted his words. I wanted to believe, but I doubted. Rick's mom had also said something similar to me during one of our many talks since I got out the hospital. It's all just so hard to wrap my mind around. Why would God have created music in nature *for me*? I could tell his mom felt sorry I had to go through what I did, but she didn't push her beliefs on me. She just hugged me.

I shook my head and looked at Rick as he sat a few paces away. I needed to do this by myself.

I sat and listened.

I sat for an hour staring at the dark blue sea and trying to hear music that eluded me. Was there really any music? And if there were, was it meant for me to hear?

Why would God allow bad things to happen?

Oh, yeah, free will. Rick's mom talked to me about this too. Part of me wishes we were robots, but humanity wouldn't like that. We…I enjoy free will. But sometimes free will stinks.

I turned my head to look at Rick, who was also sitting with eyes closed and taking in the sounds.

Pulling the hoodie over my head, I closed my eyes and tried hard to listen. With my mind's eye, I saw Daddy. He held me, a four-year old then, in his arms as he carried me onto the beach. The air was crisp, and the ocean crashed loudly against the rocks. I heard his voice. Warm tears ran down my cool cheeks as I remembered the scene vividly.

"Beautiful Sara, God gave us the skill to play and feel the music He puts in our hearts. He also placed it in nature all around us to inspire us. Whenever I go through a dry spell or a down time, I come here and I become revived. Listen, Sara. Hear the music," explained my father.

"Daddy, I only hear the crash."

"Listen closer," he said.

I listened and I could hear it.

"I hear it, Daddy."

"Great, sweetie. Things are going to get pretty busy, so I don't know if we'll be able to do this again. Promise me you won't forget what you heard today," he said.

"I promise," the four-year old me replied.

But I did forget, and here I sit frantically trying to hear the music I remembered in my head. I pulled the hoodie back off my head, letting the wind whip at my hair. I felt the breeze, but still no music. I looked out toward the ocean and then to the sky.

"Daddy, I'm sorry. I broke my promise. Please help me hear it again. God, help me hear your song."

I stood up and held my arms at my sides, with my palms facing the sea. Turning my head slightly to one side, I heard a soft whistle. I closed my eyes. The wind sounded like horns against my ears. Then, I heard the drum beat of the ocean with seagulls sounding off mini-climactic shrieking cymbals. My wind-blown hair created a rhythm of its own. Suddenly, my brain filled in the rest.

I opened my eyes again. I could hear it. I could feel it. I heard my special song, the song I heard on that beach so many years ago. I leaned forward onto my toes and inhaled deeply, infusing my insides with the music I heard.

That made me smile.

I walked over to Rick and stretched my arms out to him.

"May I have this dance?" I asked.

He tilted his head to one side, took my hands, and stood facing me. Sliding his hand behind my waist, we started to waltz on the sand. I leaned my head against his chest. After a few steps, Rick twirled me around and pulled me closer still.

When we stopped dancing, Rick kissed me gently on my lips. It felt like a dream.

"You're on your way, Sara."

"Thank you. It took a while, but I finally heard it."

I hugged him tightly.

"Let's go home," he said. Arm in arm, we walked back toward the car.

RICK'S FINAL NOTE
ଫ

Wow, it's like flying through the air when I kiss Sara. I wanted more when we were in my aunt's shed, but I knew it wouldn't be a good idea – not yet. I knew my mom and aunt would be thrilled about my decision, but I wasn't holding back for them. In some ways it was for Sara, but mostly, I did it for me. I did not want to be responsible for Sara not healing emotionally as she should.

I'm really glad I talked to Aunt Emma about Sara. I would have totally messed things up otherwise. Sara's situation is so difficult. I'm sure I would have pushed her further over the edge by saying or doing the wrong things.

I felt horrible saying the things I did. I never wanted to hurt her. Why does someone have to experience so much pain before healing can take effect?

The best thing I ever did was take Sara to the beach. It was a hunch. I didn't know it would work, but being there really reached into her soul. I think she's on her way.

I can't believe my recital is only a few days away. I'm pretty nervous about having a representative from the Julliard

School of the Arts admission office there. I can't believe they're actually coming to hear me. I can't believe they're sending someone to Cherry Hill West High School. I'm grateful to the guidance counselor for making this possible.

If it weren't for Sara joining me, I think I would lose my nerve. I'm so glad we got to practice enough so she could play with me.

ଔ

Tonight is the night of my reckoning. My gut is tied up in knots. I practiced a lot, but one wrong note, one out of place emphasis, will cost me admission to Julliard.

But tonight is not just about me. In a way, it's Sara's night of reckoning too. She seems to be doing alright, but I can't always be sure. So much has happened during the last month.

Fortunately, she picks up music quickly, so playing the right notes won't be a problem for her. Her confidence will be her challenge.

"Are you ready?" I asked as Sara walked over to me.

"I think so," she replied.

I looked at her and felt my heart beat jump just a bit. Her hair hung over her shoulders, but she pulled a portion up into a pony tail.

"You're gorgeous, Sara," I said, holding her chin up.

Sara blushed.

"You look very handsome, Rick," Sara said, looking at me with flirtatious eyes.

I felt my own face grow warm.

"I like the color of the lipstick you're wearing."

"Thanks. It's rose pink. Mom helped me pick it out."

"I'd kiss you, but I don't want to smudge or end up wearing it. Hmm. I guess I'll do this instead."

I kissed her hand, and then her forehead.

We hugged.

"Rick, thanks for this opportunity."

"Thank *you* for helping me be my best," I replied. "Do you remember the order?"

"I think so, but say it so I know for sure."

"Ok, I play four pieces, then you join me for two. First, *Linus and Lucy*, then Beethoven's Ninth Symphony. Then, you play one. By the way, what is it?"

"It's a surprise."

"Ah."

"Then you play the last song."

"Right."

I was nervous, but having Sara with me calmed my heart.

"You'll be fine, Sara."

After a few minutes, the recital began. I took my place on the stage and began to play. It came naturally for me. Many hours of practice made it effortless. I focused the nervous feelings into the adrenaline needed to stay in the zone. At the end of my fourth musical selection, the audience applauded energetically. I felt elated, no errors.

Now, it was Sara's turn.

"I want to introduce Sara, my girlfriend. She'll be playing a couple pieces with me and then one on her own."

Sara walked out onto the stage. At first, she looked frightened when she looked out at all the people. She almost hugged herself. Suddenly, she looked at me and smiled when I motioned for her to sit next to me at the piano.

"You'll do just fine. Pretend it's only us in the music room the first time we played together," I whispered.

When she finally relaxed, we started to play the song that brought us together.

Before long, it was her turn to play the violin in accompaniment to my piano performance of Beethoven's Ninth Symphony. When we finished, we bowed and I left her alone on stage for her solo performance. It sounded familiar. It took a moment before I realized that Sara played the instrumental her father wrote, but it was different somehow. She had added a part of who she is to the piece and made it her own. I knew then that Sara would be fine.

I looked out at the audience and saw how much her music had moved them. The song moved my heart too, and I felt like crying. As she played, I felt hope, and then happiness. Sara told her life's story through music and everyone understood her language.

When she finished playing, Sara beamed. My precious Sara, oh, how much you have grown.

I love you with all my heart.

MUSICAL HEALING
୫

I'm so grateful to Rick for helping me to find myself. He has no idea how much going to the beach helped me. I had forgotten how much the shore meant to me. Being there reconnected me to my father who nurtured this talent I have inside me.

Mom helped me get ready for the recital. She went shopping and picked out a dress and lipstick to match. It's been too long since she'd done something like that for me. When Mom returned home she handed me the shopping bag and combed my hair.

"Beautiful baby, you are going to be great tonight. I'm glad I finally get to hear you play. I love you with all my heart."

"I love you too, Mommy. Thanks for being here."

The first conversations I had with Mom after leaving the hospital weren't so sweet. I hated her for not doing more to protect me from her monster husband. For days, I wouldn't even let her touch me.

"Why didn't you try to stop him? Why didn't you break down the door or something?" I had said ignoring the taste of salty tears in my mouth.

"I wanted to, but I was scared. He swore if I ever tried to stop him, he would do worse. He'd kill you. I couldn't let that happen. I didn't know what else to do. My whole body hurt whenever he touched you. I wish I had the courage to do more. I wish I had your determination to look to someone else for help."

"I didn't look for Rick. He just sorta happened. You should have told me what he said. We could have escaped together. I always thought you would run back to him if I ever mentioned leaving to you. That's why I never told you about Rick."

"I'm so sorry, Sara. Please forgive me for not being a better mom. After talking with the psychologist, I now know I did more harm to us because of my fear. I'm determined to make better choices in my life, ones not made out of desperation."

Her words had meant a lot to me, but it wasn't until after the beach that I allowed Mom back into my heart. When I told Mommy I loved her, I meant it. Regaining the trust I had in her before she married Chuck would take time, but we had that now...no pressure. I would never want to lose her. I needed her close.

"I'm so glad you're here," I added. I hugged my mom, and Dontae, Elena, and Joel joined us.

"We finally got our family back, the way it was meant to be," said Dontae.

We all got ready and hurried out of the house. When we finally got to school, it took me a while to find Rick. I was happy when I saw him backstage. It's always so freeing whenever I see him. I'm glad that his love allows him to be truthful with me, even when it hurts. I think our friendship will last the long haul. I think our love will take us through the difficult times ahead.

After we went over the schedule, it was time for him to play. Rick did a superb job playing. I'm positive he'll get into Julliard. I'm so proud of him.

As I waited for my turn to arrive, I thought of the possibility of going to Julliard myself. Rick told me that's a huge possibility since I'll be playing in front of a representative tonight. I'm nervous, but I'm also excited.

When I heard my name, I walked out onto the stage. At first, the lights blinded me, but when my eyes adjusted, my heart sped into third gear at the sight of so many people. I quickly scanned the audience and found Ms. Conner and Miss Emma, but seeing them did not bring any comfort.

Fear started attacking my limbs. I felt my fingers brush against my arm in preparation for self-preservation. Who knows what my facial expression betrayed? I forgot how to smile.

Then, I saw a movement on my left and turned my head in that direction. Seeing Rick's smiling handsome face calmed me immediately. My heart resumed the light pitter patter it kept whenever he was near.

Rick beckoned me to the bench, so I smiled and floated across the stage to him. I can't recall how. After I sat next to him, Rick squeezed my hand and leaned toward my ear.

"You'll do just fine. Pretend it's only us in the music room the first time we played together," whispered Rick.

I nodded, comforted, my body starting to relax. Only then did he begin to play.

First we played my favorite Peanut's song followed by Beethoven's Ninth Symphony. Sooner than I expected, it was my turn to play...by myself. My stomach clenched as I saw Rick leave the stage. The lights dimmed with a spotlight focused on me. I inhaled deeply and tried to remember the way I felt at the beach this past weekend. I closed my eyes and the feeling of freedom filled my heart and mind. I started to play.

I can't remember playing the notes. They merely flowed from my fingers. I and the violin became one. It told my story without me having to say a word. I felt freedom in sharing my life with everyone. Perhaps, someone else could experience the hope that I finally experienced.

When I finished playing the last note, everyone gave me a standing ovation. Rick looked at me and smiled, giving me a thumbs-up. As I looked out at the audience, I realized that I did this. I played Dad's song from my heart and others loved it. They loved me playing it. I have something to offer.

No longer am I trapped by my fears. I'm not well yet, but I'm healing.

I'm so proud of myself for not giving up.

I am free to grow, to live, to love, to play, under no one's control. I feel so light and my heart is happy.

I turn 18 today, the beginning of a new life.

I have hope.

My name is Sara Miller and I am a beautiful girl.

By Cassandra Ulrich

A Beautiful Girl
a teen inspirational novella

Love's Intensity
a teen paranormal romance novel

Billiard Buddies
a New Adult romance novella

By Cassandra Skelton

Poetical Collections
Encouraging Through Sharing: A Christian's Perspective
Life Experienced
A Love Gift
Real Purpose: You Are Special